SKY SHIFTER

Caroline Pitcher likes writing books best of all. She also likes walking her dog, looking at hills and the sea, listening to music, baking cakes and making soup.

One morning, when she was looking at a hillside, she thought of a story for a picture book. It flowed on and on and became the *Year of Changes* quartet . . .

ALSO BY CAROLINE PITCHER

11 O'Clock Chocolate Cake

Mine

Silkscreen

Year of Changes quartet

Cloud Cat

CAROLINE PITCHER

SKY
SHIFTER

EGMONT

For Lisa Oakden

EGMONT
We bring stories to life

First published in Great Britain 2005
by Egmont Books Limited
239 Kensington High Street,
London W8 6SA

Text copyright © 2005 Caroline Pitcher
Illustrations copyright © 2005 David Wyatt

The moral rights of the author and the illustrator have been asserted

ISBN 1 4052 0850 3

1 3 5 7 9 10 8 6 4 2

A CIP catalogue record for this title is available from the British Library

Typeset by Avon DataSet Ltd, Bidford-on-Avon, Warwickshire
Printed and bound in Great Britain
by the CPI Group

CONTENTS

CHAPTER 1

THE SUNSHINE THIEF

Luka's mother had eyes made of silver.

He saw her in his half-dreams, smiling down at him.

'Please stay!' he begged, but she shook her head and vanished.

The dawn streamed through the skylight in the bakery roof. It woke Luka's brother, Jez. Luka heard his lips counting. *Seven…fourteen…twenty-one…*

At forty-nine, *bang*! Jez leaped out of bed and shivered for a delicious moment. At sixty-three, *crash*! he flung open the door so that the warm air from the bakery billowed up the staircase and into the attic, bringing the scents of hot bread and cinnamon.

'Can we go to the river today?' asked Luka.

'Yeah,' said Jez, scrambling into his clothes, 'when I've finished baking. Go back to sleep for now.'

Jez charged out, slammed the attic door and hurled himself downstairs three at a time.

The dog was sprawled across Luka's legs, pinning him down. He felt her paws twitch. In her sleep, she was running with a wolf pack. Luka lay and listened. He heard the river tumble from the mountains and the swallows' wings scissor as they flitted from the bakery roof to the woodshed. Downstairs, the trays packed with loaves slid into the ovens. The doors slammed shut. Big Katrin arrived for work and soon the kettle begin to whistle.

Luka dozed. From far away, he heard Dimitri chuckle and Katrin's footsteps on the cobblestones. He drifted into dreams of his Cloud Cat. He stroked her rich dappled fur. Luka and the Cloud Cat bounded through the mountains. He saw the world greedily through her gold nugget eyes, until he woke up, sweating.

Someone was at the bakery door. A hand brushed against the doorknocker.

That was all.

Jez sat at the table, thinking about eating another cinnamon bun. Luka was safe upstairs asleep in the attic, and his breakfast waited for him on a plate: two thick slices of Just For Us loaf with two curls of yellow butter.

Dimitri and Big Katrin had gone to the miller's for flour. The open door let in a long panel of sunshine. It lay across the flagstones, gleaming with the promise of fine days and the end of the fighting.

As Jez sat at the table, a shadow slid in through the door and ate up the sunshine.

The shadow swallowed Jez's happiness too. It left him with that horrible feeling he knew so well, that sense of *dread,* as if he wore a heavy belt hung with charms. The charms were made of lead. They were all the lost treasures of his childhood. The bicycle, the football, and the boots he did not have for his fourteenth birthday. That was the first birthday without his mother and father. It was the first party without his friends lost in the war. Big Katrin baked him a cake and Dimitri and Luka sang loudly, but they could not fill the empty spaces round the table.

The lead charms dragged Jez down. The only

treasure he had left was his brother, Luka.

As Jez stared at the shadow on the floor, it withdrew.

He made himself stand and walk to the door.

Nobody was there, but when he looked up the narrow street, he saw the shadow crawling away over the cobblestones.

Jez went back into the bakery and sat down. He did not want a cinnamon bun now.

He thought, I shall wait to be sure whatever it was has gone. Then I'll wake Luka. We'll go to the riverbank at the foot of the mountain.

We're all right. It was just a shadow. We're safe here in the bakery with Dimitri and Katrin.

CHAPTER 2

IN THE EAGLE'S EYE

The eagle was hunting.

Springtime spread out a picnic just for him, offering newborn goats and young hares. In the forest there were fauns. Their long legs wobbled and gave way when they tried to run from his stern yellow eye. His wings swept the air in and out, in and out, and the wind carried their rhythm down the mountainside. His shadow flew below him on the snow, a dark angel of death without eyes. As it passed, small creatures scurried for their lives.

He soared on a swell of air up into the deep blue sky and turned to gold in the sunlight.

A small face appeared in his eagle eye. The face was down on the bank by the river. It had a mouth and eyes. It was turned up to the sky, and the eagle saw another movement. There were two creatures of a similar kind. The creature with the small upturned face was Luka. And there was a third creature on the riverbank. A sandy wolf. It was no threat to *him*. The eagle was the supreme hunter of the mountains. He could catch anything that moved. *Anything*. The eagle yelped, a small high noise that carried across these spaces.

He had seen his next kill. The small face would do. He would take it, wriggling in his talons, down to his nest, where his hungry mate sat, waiting for some sweet, raw flesh.

Luka's hearing was as sharp as a cat's. He heard the rhythm of the eagle's wing-beats as clearly as a drum-roll. He heard its yelp of triumph, too.

'Jez! I just heard a dog yap. And there's a throbbing noise, like the engine of a boat.'

'Rubbish!' scoffed Jez. 'The sea is miles and miles away.'

'No. The engine is up in the sky.'

'All *I* can hear is you prattling!' said Jez. He sat up and yawned. He rubbed his eyes, and looked around. 'Ah! The sun has shifted that mist at last. I can see all the way up to the mountaintops.'

'What can you see?'

'Just a few goats running away up the rocks. Snow. And . . . wow!'

'*What*? Tell me, Jez!'

'There's a big gold bird up there in the sky. I bet it's an eagle. We saw an eagle when you were little, Luka. When you rode on the horse with Mum. Remember?'

A sharp pain twisted under Luka's ribs. He did not want to remember riding on the horse, did not want to remember sitting safe in front of his mother, sheltered by her arms, smelling the warm horse smell and patting the taut black neck. He did not want to remember listening to his mother's low voice. The memories hurt.

Jez reminisced. 'Yeah, you were on the horse, but I had to walk, and I got horrible blisters because my shoes were too small. Do you remember?'

'No. I don't. So tell me what the eagle looks like.'

'It's huge. It looks like a black cloud with the sun behind it! It's got talons like meat hooks, the ones they hang lambs and pigs on when they have been slaughtered. Dad said its beak and talons were like its knife and fork.'

Luka did not want to think about his father either, but Jez went on, 'He said it looked as if it was wearing a big pair of baggy feather trousers. The tips of its wings are edged in gold. They ripple. And it has staring golden eyes that can see for miles.'

'So it can see us all the way down here?'

'I suppose so.'

'Could it catch me, Jez?'

'Of course it could, but I'm here to look after you. A sparrow could carry *you* off. Know your place, small fry!' cried Jez, pushing Luka over on to the grass. He put his hand up to shade his eyes and watched the eagle sitting up in the sky, waiting.

'I'm going for a walk.' Jez scrambled to his feet. Luka heard him galumph along the bank, his feet crushing the wet grass. He heard the dog panting after him, and he shouted, 'Be careful of land mines, Jez!'

He tensed his body, waiting for a *boom*. There wasn't one. He listened to the river singing as it fell down from the mountains, was caught in little coves and whirled its way free again. The water played a hundred different notes and all of them were in harmony.

Deep snow had lain all winter long. Now it had melted and filled the river, almost spilling over the bank, sending it rushing towards the sea. The wind rustled in bunches of keys in the ash trees. And the birds! They were so rowdy, boasting and squabbling and fluttering at each other. In the background, over and over again, was the chorus of the cuckoo's two silly notes.

Luka heard the ground shake and the grasses break as Jez tramped back. Along with the tramping came a burning, acrid smell.

'Eugh, Jez! You stink!'

Jez sniffed his sleeve and said, 'Phew! It must be wild garlic. The bank is covered in it.'

The dog barked sharply, making them jump. Jez shouted, 'Shut up, stupid! Lie down!'

She lay next to Luka, still grumbling. Luka put out his hand to stroke her and felt the hairs on her back bristling.

'Silly old girl,' he whispered. 'There's nothing to bark at on such a beautiful day.'

The brothers sat with their faces raised to the sun,

wanting its warmth after the long winter. They closed their eyes in pleasure, loving the light beating on their eyelids.

So Jez did not see the thin figure that slipped between the trees, and Luka did not hear the twigs snap as it hid and spied on them.

CHAPTER 3

TIME TO KILL

Jez opened his eyes and blinked at a spattering of yellow stars in the grass. They were celandine flowers, opening to the sunlight.

'The springtime makes so much noise, doesn't it?' murmured Luka, head on one side. 'I don't know how people cope with seeing things as well as hearing them. There's so much going on. It's exhausting.'

Jez turned to stare at his little brother. He often said odd things, but he was getting even odder lately. Jez couldn't quite say *how* he had changed. Luka had wandered away into the snow and been lost. Jez found him in a cave, deeply asleep. Luka rested for weeks until the strength began to creep back into his body, but he was changed.

Today in the spring sunshine, Luka's face was as pale as ever. It was shaped like a slender heart framed with ragged black curls. His skin was thin and translucent. The veins under his skin were violet, as if they were the veins on a crocus.

Yet Luka was *not* fragile. There was a strength shining from inside, as if someone else was with him. *In* him, making him stronger. Jez was afraid of that strength.

'Come on,' he said, getting to his feet.

'Where are we going?'

'To the village. We'll come back soon, to see the fish swim upriver from the sea. You'll hear them splashing as they leap.' Jez grabbed Luca's arm, to start him on the way.

The eagle riding the wind current watched them move. His talons twitched. He flexed his gold-fingered wings. If his mate had to leave the nest to hunt for food, their eggs would chill and the eaglets inside would freeze to death. So it was down to him to feed them both. Now! *Time to kill.*

A threat moved into his long vision. It was a bird with

a pale head, flapping above the forest. It was approaching *his* air space and soon it would reach *his* nest.

The eagle forgot the creatures on the riverbank. His whole being concentrated on the invader. He rose on the swell of air like a dark sail ripped from a ship's mast and rode the wind.

At the last moment the pale-headed intruder saw him. It turned around. The eagle sat on the wind, watching it flap its ponderous way back across the forest.

A croak distracted him.

A crow. *It* hadn't seen him.

The eagle changed direction. He flew above the hapless crow and hovered with his wing tips trembling. He steadied himself, and fell clean as the blade of a guillotine, scooping the crow out of the sky and slicing with his hind claws. The crow's struggle was over.

Luka and Jez and the panting dog hurried on, quite unaware of the death in the sky above them, and the figure following behind them on the ground.

CHAPTER 4

BLUER THAN BLUE

'Slow down!' cried Luka. 'I haven't got long lanky legs like you. Listen . . . what's that?'

Bird song tumbled out of the sky as if someone was pouring silver from a jug.

'It's a skylark,' said Jez. 'It's so high I can't see it.'

Luka stood, listening to the skylark, thinking that anything singing so joyfully might burst apart. He said, 'Imagine being up in the sky!'

'Imagine flying vertically like that, straight up from the ground!' shivered Jez, remembering black planes that passed over the village when the occupation began. One of them had landed on the cliffs above the sea. It crouched like a great dung beetle and then roared straight up into the air until it had disappeared.

They had stopped by a thicket of thorn bushes. It was an ancient hedge, run wild in the war because nobody had time to cut it. Buds as round as pearls clung to the rough black twigs between the thorns.

'Hey, Luka, there's a secret world under here! Mouse mazes, rabbit catacombs, and queen bees' castles. There's treasure too . . . I can smell it. Mmm!'

In the dark thicket shone a crown of brilliant blue spears. The colour was intense. It must have come from another dimension. The smell of the flowers was almost too sweet and Jez just had to have them! He crouched down and struggled into the thicket, cursing, and went into a frenzy, snapping every stem his hand touched.

'What are you DOING in there!' shouted Luka. 'Come on OUT!'

Jez did not hear him. In the middle of the closed thicket, the blue-green scent was heady. He snapped away. Soon he was scratched and bloodied. The thorns tore at his back. His toe caught in a root and he stumbled and swore at a cord twisted around his ankle. *Ivy*.

Jez saw that it gripped his leg with strong little suckers. He dragged the ivy cord away from his ankle and tore himself out of the thicket. As he staggered away he bumped against a tree. Vines of creeping ivy engulfed its whole trunk.

'There's a tangle of serpents swarming over this tree,' said Jez. 'They've strangled it.'

'Where? Let me see!' cried Luka. He stuck his fingers through the snaking ivy and touched the tree's bark. Then he opened his arms to cuddle the tree and felt his way round it. Jez heard the soft sound of something falling as Luka vanished. He reached into the tree trunk and grabbed his brother's arm.

'Foof! It's all cloudy sawdust!' spluttered Luka, wiping his face.

'That's because it's rotten, Luka!' shouted Jez. 'I do wish you'd be careful. Now, hold out your hand.' He closed Luka's hand around a mass of flower stalks.

'*Mmm*, lovely! They smell like heaven,' said Luka. 'But the ends of the stalks are all slimy and sappy. I hope they look better than they feel. What are you going to do with them?'

'They're bluebells. I'll take them to the orphanage for the children. '

Luka snorted with laughter. He knew that Jez really wanted to give the flowers to Imogen. Tall Imogen, with the skin soft as an apricot, and the long plait of hair. She worked at the orphanage.

Luka bent his face down to the flowers until his senses were drenched by their sweet scent. 'What kind of blue are these bells?' he asked.

'*Blue* blue. Intense. Violet. More blue than blue . . . They are unreal. Hey, *I* can't describe it, Luka! What do you think I am? A poet?'

'No!' said Luka. 'Definitely not.'

The brothers set off again towards the village.

The eagle sailed down to his nest with the crow pinioned in his talons.

The thin figure followed the brothers, keeping out of sight. It darted under the thorn bushes, then out again. It picked up a fallen flower and held it to its face for a moment. Sniffed it. Coughed and spluttered. Threw the flower down, whispering, *'Idiot.'*

CHAPTER 5

THE END OF
THE STORY

J ez strode through the village with Luka trotting close,
bumping against him every now and then. The dog ran
with them, froth gathering around her pink tongue.

In the long winter, snow had cast a spell over the war-
battered village, turning it into a fairytale land of castles
and towers. When the snow melted, it gave away its secret;
this magic land was made of ruined houses after all. It was
a dump. Broken chairs, smashed bottles and cups from
crumbled kitchens lay among the stones, ready to cut the
children who longed to play there.

The brothers disappeared round a corner. Out of a
glassless window peered the face of their pursuer. It was

Simlin, the son of Vaskalia who lived in the little five-sided house outside the village. On Simlin's forehead flamed an orange birthmark shaped like a scorpion, with its stinging tail arched over its back. Simlin was not used to daylight. He blinked watery eyes and shaded them with his long hand.

Jez, Luka and the panting dog arrived at a big door peppered with bullet holes. Years ago, this building had been the school. Now it was the orphanage, full of children from the village and the countryside roundabout.

Jez took the flowers from Luka's arms and dropped them in the porch.

As soon as they walked into the big room, the children ran towards Luka. They grabbed his hands, stroked his hair, hugged him and planted noisy kisses on his cheek.

Eva, who ran the orphanage with Imogen, was pouring drinks. She turned, and Jez saw a smile break out across her face. It seemed to him that he had not seen her smile for years. And then Imogen hurried across the room towards them and Jez's heart missed a beat. She picked up Luka and swung him into the air.

'It's wonderful to see you up and about, Luka!' she

cried. 'You look great! Jez, you've really nursed him well.'

Jez's face burned with pleasure so he looked away, fast.

'But you need to fatten up a bit, Luka,' she said.

'*Me*? But just look at my brother with his weedy muscles!'

'Tease! You're still light as a feather,' said Imogen. 'Don't tell me Big Katrin has stopped baking her cakes?'

'I'm just made so small and neat, Imo!' cried Luka.

'You *do* look very funny!' squealed Aidan-who-had-to-be-carried-everywhere. 'You have not grown at all. In fact, I think you've shrunk. And your face is whiter than ever. But of course, I forgot! You can't see yourself in a mirror, can you?'

Aidan lunged forward on his chair, grabbed Luka's hand and squealed, 'C'mon, tell us all about it! We want to know exactly where you've been without us!'

Luka reached both hands up to Aidan's face and felt his bunched-up cheeks. Aidan was smiling, so maybe he was not scheming to do something nasty.

'I'll tell you all about it,' he said. 'Sit down, Aidan.'

'I can't do anything else without any legs!' crowed Aidan, as Imogen wedged cushions around him to keep him from falling.

Jez fetched a chair and set it down on to the threadbare rug, guiding Luka to it. The children thundered across the groaning floorboards, climbed over each other and squabbled to sit nearest to Luka, looking up at him expectantly. Jez looked at their small, pale, ancient faces. These children had already seen so much death and sorrow. Their faces were shadowed by mistrust.

There was a cry from the other end of the room. '*Mee tooo!*' Eva hurried over to an iron cot in the corner where a little boy with eyes like a hare was shaking the iron bars. He held up his arms. Eva lifted him out. He kicked at her until she set him down on the floor. Then he dashed towards the children on all fours.

The last child to arrive was Maria, stone deaf since her house and family had been set alight by men from the valley to the east. They had set fire to the gas canister and watched the house burn, but in the end someone had taken pity and rescued Maria.

Imogen went to stand next to Jez. She wrinkled her nose and said, 'Phew, Jez! Can I smell onions on you? Has Dimitri decided to cook stew today?'

Jez's smile faded. 'It's wild garlic.'

Luka perched on the chair, gripping the seat with both hands and swinging his thin legs. Now that the time had come to tell his story, all those feelings came back, all those emotions he had felt out in the snow. Dread, joy, fear and exhilaration.

'Come on, Luka! Get on with it,' ordered Aidan in his fat voice. '*Once upon a time . . .*'

'I wanted to go off into the snow,' began Luka. His voice trembled. 'I was fed up of being indoors. Sick of darkness and banging into walls. I kept having dreams about somewhere else. So . . . I hid in my grandfather's old blanket chest. I closed it up. The old bus came. I heard it stop. The driver knocked on the door but I still hid, and the bus went away again. Good! I waited till its chugging was gone down the hill, and then I lifted the lid, crept downstairs and opened the back door . . . and . . .'

'Why? What was there?' cried the children.

'He doesn't know because he's blind,' stated Aidan. 'Aren't you? Dead-eye-Luka!'

'So what if I am blind? Mr No Legs! Half-a-boy-Aidan!'

'Peppermint eyes! Boiled sweet eyes! You were naughty, Luka. Why did you go off on your own?'

'Because I wanted to! I wanted to go wherever I could. I wanted to find out if it was as exciting as my dream.'

'And was it?' shrilled Aidan, squirming in his cushions.

'Yes! It was fantastic!'

Jez saw his little brother's shining face and felt his heart sink.

Luka was sure of his story now and he loved telling it. He stood up and cried, 'First, I crawled over the snow in the yard. Then I thought, That's silly, you're crawling on all fours like the dog! So I stood up and walked on my two legs. Like this . . . I was following –' He hesitated. 'I walked for miles and miles. It was so snowy and cold. Someone stood next to me but it was a post. There was a swaying bridge and winds that tried to snatch me off and throw me down into the Depths of Lumb. There was –' Luka hung his head. When he raised it again he said, 'I'm not telling you what there was down there. I'm not telling you the whole story because some of you will be frightened.'

'Tell us, Luka, tell us!' screamed the children.

'I got lost. I fell down and down a horrible chasm. I heard monsters slithering deep down under the earth.

They were in the darkest place of all.'

'Did the monsters try to eat you?' screeched Aidan, thumping his chair in excitement.

'I tried and struggled and in the end I got away from them. I had to rest . . . and then I began to climb.'

The story was too much for some of the children. Michael squirmed across the rug on his tummy and pulled himself up on to Eva's lap. Eleni wrapped her arms tight round herself and began to rock forwards and backwards, and Florin cradled his block of wood and whispered, *bang . . . bang . . . dead . . .*

Luka's voice became stronger. His face flushed pink and his sightless eyes moved fast from side to side in his excitement.

'I climbed and climbed.' He pawed the air to show how he did it. 'Think how I felt!'

'Cold?' cried Lisa.

'Yes. I thought I might freeze into an icicle and have to stay there forever, hanging from a rock.'

'Starving hungry!' screeched Aidan.

Jez said loudly, 'No, Luka wasn't hungry because I had packed him lots of food for his dinner. He had sandwiches and apples he was going to bring here. You ate up every bit, didn't you, Luka?'

'Yes, but I didn't eat it all myself!' said Luka and turned his face away with that secret little smile that irritated Jez and made him remember his father's words, *If you fall down into the Depths of Lumb, you'll never come out the same* . . .

'*Then* what happened?' bawled Aidan.

'I played –' Luka stopped and sucked in his breath. His face tightened and he could not go on.

Imogen said, 'It's a wonderful story, Luka. But you must be careful what you tell, because some of us *are* a bit frightened.'

'But we haven't finished yet!' screeched Aidan, his face red and tight with envy. 'That's not the end of the story, Luka. You have not told us what is deep down at the bottom of the Depths of Lumb. And *I* think you are very badly behaved to go off by yourself!'

'I wasn't by myself,' said Luka, but Aidan was too incensed to hear him.

He shouted, '*And* you behaved like a big baby! You went miles and miles and up and up but you never went right down and down, did you? And –'

'Aidan!' cried Imogen. 'Stop it. Luka, you're getting such a good storyteller. I'm going to paint some pictures of what you've told us, like I did of your dream.'

'Humph!' came a bad-tempered snort.

Luka turned his face towards the sound. 'Didn't you like the story, Aidan?'

'No, because you haven't told us everything, have you?' sneered Aidan. 'Coward!'

'AIDAN!' shouted Imogen, but his face was pink with excitement now and he babbled, 'The landmine that blew me up was called a Pineapple! That was its shape, a special kind! So there, Luka! The Pineapple Mine was made far away. In *another land*! It was made to blow up a big tank but it blew my legs off instead, and threw lots of splinter bits all over the place *and* killed my parents. So there! So there!'

Luka felt the blood of embarrassment rushing up to his face. Damn Aidan! Why did he always put his finger on the bit that hurt?

Aidan perched on his pile of cushions. His arms were folded. His lip was curled in disdain. His empty trouser legs dangled beneath his body. He announced, 'You never went down *there* in the earth. Not down to the darkest place. You never went to meet those slimy slithering monsters under the earth, because you're scared of ghosts, aren't you? My mother and father are ghosties now and so are yours! Where's your dad, Luka? Is he under the ground? Is he a ghost?'

Sadness rose up in Luka's chest. He swallowed hard. He said, 'I shall not go to the Depths of Lumb again. I decided I shan't go deep into the ground again.'

'Because you're frightened, aren't you, Luka? You're frightened!'

There was a sickening crunch as the ceiling split open. Plaster and rubble rained down from above.

Aidan disappeared.

CHAPTER 6

COLLAPSE!

S ilence.

'Walk to the side of the room. All of you!' said Imogen.

The children did as they were told, feeling their way through the whirling dust. They were too shocked to cry.

Imogen cried 'Someone's missing!'

'*I'm* missing,' said Luka calmly, still on his chair. 'I can't see where I am supposed to go.'

'And *I* am still on my cushions! Eva? Imogen? Get me now! My head hurts and my mouth is full of rubble!'

'You look like a statue up on a plinth, Aidan,' said Eva, parting his hair and finding a cut.

Jez stood by Luka, trying not to laugh.

'Do I look funny then?' asked Luka.

'Yes! Like a grubby little snowman.'

Luka tried to smile. The falling ceiling had given him a shock, but there was worse. He had heard that whispering again, '*Idiot. Saphead. Moonraker. Idiot.*' He thought it had stopped since his journey into the snow. He was *not* an idiot.

'There's still somebody missing!' cried Imogen. 'There should be thirteen, with Luka – where is the other one?'

In the centre of the room there still hung a dusty cloud. As it settled, they saw a little figure, drenched in fallen plaster. *Maria.* Imogen hurried to her and brushed the dust away from her eyes and mouth with her hand. She knelt in front of her and signed with her hands 'Are you all right?' Maria blinked and nodded.

'EUGH!' Aidan began to spit, hard, to rid his mouth of dust. Soon they were all at it.

Jez stared up at the gape in the ceiling. 'The rafters must have shifted. It was that bomb that got Eva's house,' he said. 'It shook everything up. Destabilised it.' The orphans nodded at Jez's big word. It made them feel better.

'Every *day* I think the floor will cave in, or the old

electrics will burn the house down,' said Imogen. 'And now this! I must keep them safe. What shall I do?'

Jez looked down at Imogen's distraught face and his heart lurched. Usually she was calm and clear as a glassful of water.

He said, 'It's what shall *we* do, Imogen. They're not just your responsibility. They're everybody's. I'll find wood to cover up the hole. After that . . . erm . . . we know that this building has needed mending for years, and . . .'

'Be quiet, you two!' squealed Aidan angrily. 'I want Luka to finish his story! And why has the roof waited all this time to fall down? Perhaps there's a big fat king rat living up there!'

'Shhhh, Aidan,' scolded Imogen. 'You'll frighten the little ones.'

Aidan chortled with glee. He was not frightened of scuttling rats. He was always up out of the way in someone's arms or up in a chair. Giant rats wouldn't clamber over *him*.

Yet Luka felt sorry for Aidan. He sensed that Aidan was desperate to hear the end of the story. Luka could not tell the end to anybody. It was dangerous knowledge.

He had a secret gift.

The secret gift filled him with excitement and terror.

CHAPTER 7

THROUGH THE HOLE
IN THE ROOF

Simlin waited, motionless as a sleeping bat, long after the ceiling collapsed. If they heard a single soft sound, they would look up and discover him.

He heard the brothers bickering. The big one wanted to leave. The blind boy was trying to find something. Simlin heard a cupboard door open, heard him rooting around inside, making everything fall out on to the floor. *'Idiot. Pest.'*

At last. *Goodbye.* Simlin took a deep breath and spun, fast as an acrobat in a circus. He hooked his long feet over the rafter and hung there, swaying gently. Now that the big hole had happened he could see even better.

These children were altogether round a table, except one boy who crouched by the door with a piece of wood, making *rat-at-tat-boom* noises and hissing 'Dead!'

The women sliced apples into crescent moons and fetched drinks. Simlin could see steam from the mugs. Someone laughed, even though the ceiling had come down.

The fat squealing boy was being carried, cuddled up, all close to the pretty woman with the long plait of hair. A sob rose in Simlin's thin chest. *Ugly half-boy with the big bulging eyes gets cuddled. So lucky!*

He swallowed hard, and stifled the sob. It hurt! A whimper sneaked out. *Careful.* He squeezed his eyes tight shut and waited, but nobody had heard him. They were too busy with each other to notice *him*. Simlin had often been here, climbing up the outside of the orphanage as if his feet were sticky like a fly's feet. It had been easy to pull some loose tiles off the roof and squeeze in, wriggle across the rafters, and work away, gouging out that spy-hole in the ceiling, and today the spy-hole had made itself even bigger.

This was Simlin's favourite thing: spying. Especially spying on the people down there.

He heard the pretty woman call, 'The sun's still shining. Let's go for a walk and look at the springtime. We can find some flowers. Open the door, please, Florin. Florin, *please* stop shooting us.'

The other woman carried Lazy-Boy-No-Legs to the door and opened it.

'There are flowers all over the floor of the porch already,' squealed Lazy-Boy-No-Legs. 'Blue ones! All limp and squishy.'

Simlin heard all their little feet trotting, the door slam shut and the rafters tremble. Then silence. *Alone.*

That blind boy wasn't with the children going to see the springtime. He had gone somewhere else with the big bully brother.

The orphanage was not the only place that Simlin had watched the blind boy. He looked for him in his mother's glass seeing-ball when Vaskalia was asleep. Lately the glass ball had been disappointing. Even when Simlin wiped away the grease and soot, he couldn't see anything. It was empty. The boy had been trapped in there with that big shadow creature with shoulder blades as big as axes, but not now. Why could Simlin only see him in there *sometimes*?

Never mind. Today Simlin had spied on the boy, his brother and their dog, down by the river. Still did not know what it was the blind boy had…what did Mother want with him . . .?

Simlin gripped the rafter tightly and lurched forwards, arms out as if he were on a trapeze. He dangled there, swinging backwards and forwards, gazing down into the orphanage.

A shaft of sunlight came in high from a window. Simlin saw specks of dust turning in the sunlight, all gold! He gazed into the room wistfully. No Mother smells down *there*. No thick soot. No bits of gristle or skeletons on the floor. Look at all their chairs and cots and table with the little cups and plates. Look at the toys, the wooden building bricks, the tricycle and the soft bears!

He swung his body up and wriggled back, quick as a lizard, across the rafters. Two little birds flew twittering around his head. They had made a nest for their babies, all lined with soft down. Four white speckled eggs.

Simlin put the eggs in his pocket to eat later. Out on the roof he stretched up and gazed around him at the spring world. That blind boy would never see all this lovely spring coming. Ha! He shimmied down to the street and ran out of the village as fast as his skinny feet could carry him.

When the five-sided house came into sight, Simlin skidded to a stop. He remembered the plan he had made when the seeing-ball was rolling away down the road to the sea: *Get power that blind boy has, get power for self. Then Mother will love Simlin.*

He also thought, If Mother did get idiot blind boy, Simlin might live with the pretty women and the toys.

CHAPTER 8

RAINING MUD

Luka sat on a chair in the yard in the afternoon sun. He turned the drum round in his hands. He felt the creatures carved lightly into its wood. Smooth skin was stretched tightly across the drum. He tapped it. The sound from this drum he had found in the cupboard was deeper than the note from its sister drum, the one that had drummed him away with the Cloud Cat. That drum had been his most beloved thing. Where *was* it now?

He must guard this one with his life.

Something landed on his hand. He stopped drumming and searched around but couldn't find anything. There! It happened again, light on his face. It bounced away like a tiny ball. Another one! Now a few together, like raindrops, but not wet.

It stopped again. Luka heard Dimitri come bustling outside, and the sound of a tin prised open. He smelled paint. The baker burst into song and made him jump.

'I don't remember the last time I heard you singing, Dimitri!' cried Luka. 'I love it!'

Dimitri laughed. 'It *was* long ago. I can't even remember the words. Listen to the swallows. They make much better music.' Luka heard the singing of the swallows as they whizzed forwards and backwards from the wood store.

'They're like little steely-blue anchors. Red faces and round eyes all dewy...I love them! But their nests are in a mess after last winter. They've started mud-plastering.'

'So *that's* it!' cried Luka. 'The swallows are dropping mud on me!'

'And I don't blame them!' teased Jez from the doorway. 'Hey, Luka, Katrin wants you. In you go.' Luka took his drum and disappeared inside.

'Oh no . . . what's this?' roared Dimitri, reaching up to pull a bunch of wizened flowers away from the doorknocker. 'A bad wish posy. Look at it! Hexwort . . . Witch's thimbles . . . Belladonna . . . I think Vaskalia has been here!'

He threw the posy down and ground it under his boot, twisting his heel until it was just yellow powder. Taking up his brush he began to work blue paint all over the door, while streams of sweat ran down his dark face.

Jez stared down at the yellow powder that had been Vaskalia's posy of hate. It changed everything. A sombre mood settled over the bakery. Jez wanted that mood dispersed and banished. Things had to get better.

He took a deep breath and said, 'That is going to be the best door in the village, Dimitri. I wish I could fix the orphanage that easily. Poor children.'

'Why don't you get Imogen to bring them for breakfast tomorrow?' said Dimitri.

'What, *all* of them?'

'Yes, *all* of them. I'll ask Katrin to make sugar buns.'

'They'll love it!' said Jez. From inside the bakery he heard Luka's voice calling the cat 'Syrup? Syrup!' and remembered what he had come out to ask.

'Dimitri . . . Listen . . . I know you and Katrin always

keep an eye on Luka, but I'm *really* worried about him. He's changed. He's different since he came back from that cave.'

Dimitri shrugged. 'He seems much happier and full of life to me, Jez. Don't forget that he's come through a difficult time.'

'Maybe you're right,' said Jez doubtfully. He changed the subject. 'Could I leave him with you while I get some wood from our old house?'

'Of course you can.'

'I want to cover the hole in the orphanage ceiling. Suppose more of it falls down and really hurts someone?'

Supposing it falls on Imogen, before I'm brave enough to tell her how beautiful she is?

CHAPTER 9

SPIT-SPATTER-SIZZLE

Next morning, Luka placed his drum on the table and gave it a loving pat. Dimitri was giving his door another coat of paint. Jez was tidying up after the morning's baking and Big Katrin was cooking Luka's breakfast. He sat down and listened to the butter spit-spatter in the pan and two eggs being cracked on the edge of the bowl. He heard the pinch of salt, half a turn from the pepper grinder, and the whisk beating the eggs in the bowl. The bowl tipped, the beaten eggs slid into the hot butter and made it sizzle.

The loaf sighed as Katrin's knife sliced though it. The smell made Luka's mouth water. He heard the spreading of soft butter and the twist of the jam pot lid, releasing the scent of blackberry jam.

Syrup the cat landed on his knee. Luka felt bendy-soft needles pricking his leg when a couple of her kittens hauled themselves up after her. A rough tongue licked his hand. Luka stroked the cat and kittens, with first one hand, then another, paddling faster and faster. He felt the tiny shivers of the kittens' purr and Syrup's deep vibration, right through her body.

Luka chuckled as he imagined the dappled Cloud Cat bounding on to his knee. *She* would flatten him! *She* would take his skin off with her great rough tongue. Her cat smell would make his eyes water.

Cloud Cat. His secret. He shivered as he thought of her. For a moment the bakery disappeared and Luka was up in the mountains once again with her. The children at the orphanage would not understand how he could change and become part of her. He could hardly begin to understand it himself.

It was his gift.

That long winter had smothered so much. Now the world was spinning on its way once more, and the energy was in Luka's veins, too, waiting for his next change. Luka did not know what that change would be, but he knew he could do it.

Katrin placed the plate of eggs and toast in front of Luka. He ate his breakfast slowly, still in his dream. He stayed dreaming as she placed a towel around his shoulders and began snipping away at his hair.

Then the children arrived.

CHAPTER 10

ICED FINGERS

Of course, it was Aidan. He *would* be the one to do it. All the other children tiptoed carefully past the shining blue door on their way to their special breakfast.

Except Aidan. He lunged forward from Eva's arms, pressed both hands hard on the door and squealed with glee. *'Sticky sticky!'*

Dimitri said, through gritted teeth, 'Luckily for you, Aidan, I've got a bottle of turpentine out in my wood store. Now I'm going to have to paint the door all over again!' He stomped out. Aidan peeped over Eva's shoulder and stuck out his tongue at the baker's angry back.

The children's eyes grew round as they breathed in the

scent of cinnamon and freshly baked bread. They stared at Luka sitting with the towel around his shoulders. Big Katrin smiled at them and swept up the wild dark curls from the floor. She set the dustpan down by the door to empty later.

They scrambled on to chairs and their mouths began to water as Katrin sliced up a plait of bread. She handed each child a hunk to dip into the bowl of amber honey. She shook her head at Aidan, reaching out from Eva's arms.

'Give me some bread!' Aidan's crumpled face turned puce.

'Not with your hands covered in paint,' said Imogen.

'I hate you!' spat Aidan.

'Calm down and behave yourself!' said Dimitri, returning with the turpentine to clean Aidan's hands. 'There . . . now show them to Katrin.'

Aidan glowered. He held out his clean hands to Katrin. She took them, turned them over and nodded. Only then was Aidan positioned at the table, high on sacks of flour, to scoff bread and runny honey. Katrin fetched buns topped with glossy white icing, which had dribbled down their plump golden sides. She had made two each for everybody who could manage them, and everybody could, except Imogen.

'What's the matter?' asked Jez and she turned to him with wide brown eyes that made his toes curl inside his boots.

'I just don't know how I'm going to keep on looking after the children. There's hardly any money for their food, let alone for clothes and toys. But thank you for fixing that hole in the ceiling, Jez.'

Dimitri reached across the table and tore off the end of the loaf. He said, 'The warlords should compensate us for all the damage they've done.' He plunged his bread into the honey. 'They've forgotten about us. They expect us to help ourselves.'

Aidan piped up, 'But how can we help ourselves, Mr Baker? We have no mothers and fathers. We have no money. Maria can't hear. Luka can't see. Some of us are missing bits of brain, and some of us haven't even got legs.'

'There are other ways of getting things,' said Luka.

Jez frowned at him and then leaped up, shouting, 'Of course there are! When I was looking for Luka, I made snowshoes from bark. I made glasses to stop snow blindness. I could start a business. Snowshoes and snow glasses, they'll make money!"

There was a silence. Just Maria humming, and munching sounds from the children.

Imogen was the one to say it. Gently.

'Jez . . . the winter is over. There isn't any snow except high in the mountains. People might want to buy snow-shoes and snow glasses next winter, but not now.'

Jez's face flushed. 'I forgot,' he mumbled, sitting down again.

'You're good with your hands, Jez. I'm sure you could make something to sell,' said Dimitri with his mouth stuffed so full that Aidan squealed, 'Mr Baker! There is honey dribbling all down your chin. *Deesgusting*! Have you always been a baker?'

'Not always,' began Dimitri. 'For a few years I –'

'I want to buy proper beds and throw away those rusty old cots!' said Imogen. 'We need a wheelchair for Aidan, a hearing aid for Maria, and Elli, you need a new dress . . . you all need shoes . . . books . . . paper and things for colouring . . . how can we get them?'

'There's something I can't quite remember at the back of my mind,' murmured Jez. 'Something I've seen recently. Luka, when you ran away, which way did you go?'

Luka sighed. 'Out of the back door, across the yard and up the hillside.'

'Yes, but which *way*?'

'You have forgotten I can't see. You followed me, so why can't you remember the way?'

'Luka, *you* have forgotten that the world was covered in snow so that everywhere looked the same.'

'Did it?'

'Are you trying to make me angry? What happened in the Depths of Lumb?'

Luka turned his face away. He stared towards the oven range and would not say anything.

'*Luka!*'

Dimitri said, 'Don't nag him like that, Jez.'

Jez remembered what Imogen had told him: When you feel that rage rushing over you, name seven special things. He turned away and thought, She likes flowers. Bluebell, celandine, forget-me-not, buttercup, stitchwort . . .

But this time it did not calm Jez down. He did not

want to finish his breakfast. That feeling of dread returned to his stomach. Something momentous had happened to his brother Luka. *What*? Would it happen again?

CHAPTER 11

A BASKET OF CHERRIES

The bakery was quiet. The children had fallen asleep, face down in the crumbs. Only Aidan and Luka stayed awake. Aidan perched high like a king among the flour sacks, and Luka sat daydreaming of his Cloud Cat.

'Nothing is right in this land,' whispered Eva. 'I heard about the old clock in the city. The one with figures that whirr round at midnight. It's stuck! There's just Death carrying his scythe, disease and people fighting.' She shivered.

'There's more to life than that!' said Dimitri. He stood up and stretched. 'Time to get on with it.'

Imogen whispered, 'Wake up,' in Lisa's ear. Lisa stirred

and smiled, and then Imogen gently shook Maria's shoulder. The little girl jumped and gave a wailing cry, without opening her eyes.

'I don't *want* to *go*!' announced Aidan.

'Katrin and I will walk back with you,' said Dimitri. He scooped Aidan out of his throne of sacks and hugged him, chuckling, 'Little trouble-maker!'

'Forgive me?' squealed Aidan.

'*This* time,' growled Dimitri.

When they'd gone, Luka made a cradle of his arms on the table and rested his head lightly on his drum. He tried to dream himself back to the Cloud Cat. Jez interrupted his reverie, saying, 'You look pale again. Why don't you go and have a sleep?'

'I think I will,' said Luka and felt his way to the stairs.

Jez began cleaning up. He wiped the top of the range, scooping crumbs and flour into his hand. If I could earn money to help build a new orphanage, Imogen would think I was fantastic.

He heard a small noise on the doorstep. That shadow slid across the floor.

The dog growled. She slunk towards the door, and

stopped, one paw raised, eyes fixed on the squat figure in the doorway.

'Don't tell me that lazy good-for-nothing baker is out again?' crowed Vaskalia.

Dark foxes lay around her shoulders. The foxes had pointed snouts and limp paws. Their fur was mangy, and around their staring glass eyes the skin was bare. Vaskalia had scarves wrapped around her head too. She had left a slit for her eyes. They bulged like gobstoppers, veined with red and blue. They looked in different directions.

'Why don't you call off your dog?' she whined.

Jez snapped his fingers and the dog slunk back to him.

'I have come all this way, bearing gifts for the poor blind boy. I have brought him cherries. I know he likes them. Take them!'

She thrust the basket at Jez. It was covered with a filthy patterned cloth. Yet a sweet smell wafted up. Jez licked his lips.

'Aren't you going to ask me inside?' whined Vaskalia.

'We've no bread left. And it's not *my* bakery.' Jez willed Dimitri to hurry back from the orphanage.

Vaskalia's chameleon eyes fixed on Jez's face. She

cupped a hand to her mouth as if she were his conspirator, sharing a secret with him, and said, 'Dimitri would expect you to ask me inside. He is one of my admirers. You know, he longs to ask for my hand in marriage, but he cannot find the courage.'

Jez wanted to laugh, but he was scared and it came out as a spluttering raspberry. Her eyes wheeled round him. She was considering him, weighing him up. Jez's face burned red and the worm of warning began to wriggle in his stomach. *Dread* . . .

She said slyly, 'Do you know who *I* saw?'

Jez looked away down the street, but he could not move. She was watching his face. She said, '*I* saw your mother.'

'*Where?*'

'I saw her in the city. In a window. Past the market. Near the castle. Down a little winding way, at the top of a tall timbered house.'

'My mother is gone. And you don't know her!' cried Jez.

'Oh, but I do, I do! I knew her long ago. And it *was* your mother! I saw her hand. Do you remember it?'

Of course Jez remembered his mother's hand. It was almost his first memory. It had been his fault. When he was still small, Jez was lured to the range by pretty steam and a delicious fruity smell. His mother turned just in time to see him reaching for the jam pan. She grabbed it out of his reach, sending crimson jam splashing on to her hand. Little Jez was frightened by her screams and joined in, wailing. His mother smiled and shushed him and plunged her hand into cold water. After that, whenever he traced the scar and tried to kiss the red scald, she assured him it was better.

Jez hated this woman for saying she had seen his mother, *hated* her! His mother was gone, years ago, soon after his father.

'Well, well! Look what the cat's brought in! It's VaskalEEEa!' growled Dimitri, returning at last with Big Katrin. 'What are you doing so far from home? Those bad spirits will be coming down the chimney while you're out.'

'My son is at home. He will keep my cottage safe,' she twittered. She rolled one of her eyes back towards Jez.

Her son. Of course. With a shock, Jez remembered Simlin, who whispered spiteful things about Luka, so that Jez smacked him hard across the face and thought, That's that! until this woman had turned up at the school gate. She twisted Jez's wrist and spat on to his foot so that an orange blister grew there.

Dimitri snapped, 'Today's bread has all gone, madam!'

'It's not bread I want,' she said, fluttering her crusty eyelashes at Dimitri. 'I am here with gifts for the blind boy. I have brought my very best, reddest cherries. All for him!'

Again she thrust the basket at Jez. He backed away, shaking his head, and instead Big Katrin took it. Vaskalia's face puckered with rage. There was no way she could get past Katrin, so she announced haughtily, 'I have urgent business at home,' and stepped out into the street again. As she turned her foot knocked against the dustpan full of Luka's curls. She gave Jez a questioning glare, then went on her way.

Big Katrin fetched her wooden spoon with the long handle. She gingerly raised the filthy cloth that covered the basket and frowned. It was spring, far too early in the year for cherries, but there they were, plump and shiny as beetle backs, and dredged with stuck sugar. Katrin put her head down to the basket and sniffed.

With her face this close, she saw a little movement in the middle.

Quick as a wink, Katrin jerked back her head and threw the cloth over again.

What to do? This hoard of poison would never burn. Katrin looked around the yard. Most of it was concreted over, except for a little patch of earth near the wall where snowdrops and a few daffodils had braved their way through in the early spring.

She looked over the wall at the hillside. That would do. She found what she was looking for in the wood store and let herself out through the gate.

She began to dig a hole. Burial was the only way.

After digging for a few minutes, Katrin rested on the spade and looked around her. She gasped. Tiny yellow flowers were growing below the back window of the bakery. They hadn't been there yesterday.

Groundsel. It grew on witch's piss. Big Katrin pictured Vaskalia squatting on Dimitri's land to pee streams of wickedness. Like a lynx marking its territory, thought Katrin.

Her stomach heaved.

May was a bad month for old magic, but it had met its match in Big Katrin. She buried the basket and shovelled the earth heavily back on top. Nothing could climb out of *there*.

Tonight she would salt the earth all around to cleanse it. In a day or two she would plant a thorn bush and forget-me-nots close to the bakery to protect Dimitri and the brothers.

And she mustn't forget to clean up that disgusting blob of orange spittle on the doorstep.

Vaskalia waited, just out of sight. She watched Katrin begin to dig. Then she crept back towards the bakery door. Pinching her thumb and forefinger together, she took Luka's hair from the dustpan. She tucked the curls under the dead foxes, and scuttled away through the village with her head down and her shadow crawling behind her. She did not want to be seen. Some villagers shouted things at her, and if they were feeling really brave, they threw old cabbages. She hated them. But it was *her* village; she was born in the pentangle house on the edge of it and she would never leave, nor would she give up her claim on that blind boy.

On the road out towards the sea, Vaskalia saw the smoke belching from her house. She stomped through the garden, opened the door and screeched, 'Stop burning all that wood, milksop! A small fire is all we need to stop them coming down the chimney!'

Simlin scurried into the corner, sending a dish clattering. He flung his arms up in front of his face. Would she notice the pan he'd used to cook the little eggs he had taken from the orphanage roof? He'd scoured it hard with a pumice stone.

But Vaskalia had other things on her mind. She felt about on the high shelf. Her dolls' cold eyes stared at her hand in its fingerless mittens. It closed round the seeing-ball and lifted it right in front of her face.

'Nothing, nothing!' she whined. 'Where has he gone?' She whirled round at Simlin. 'Why have I just got you instead, you prince of disappointment?'

Simlin's scorpion mark flamed livid orange, but he thought, Not going to tell you I have seen the blind boy. Not going to tell you I've been out. Secret! Simlin's own secret!

He heard the *groan-ping* of the bedsprings as she bounced on to her bed, and the shuffle of the curtains as she tugged them around herself. She chuntered, 'When the market starts, I'll sell my plants, and spells and potions, and buy me a fine strong donkey.'

Why does she want a donkey? wondered Simlin.

Vaskalia stopped chuntering. Simlin heard her hiding something under her pillow. He longed for her to fall asleep. It was hard to tell when she slept, because the little house with five sides was always full of sounds. The fire in the middle of the floor hissed like a dragon as it crawled over dank green logs. There was shifting and whistling from up on the beams where Bone Cracker the vulture shifted from foot to scaly foot. It stretched its big wings and flapped them as if it was shaking out a coat.

Simlin heard sagging, boinging and clattering, as his mother rolled around on her fat mattress. He heard her gnawing at the copper bangles round her wrist. Spitting, then green explosions bursting in the fire. At last he heard snorts and snuffles as she slept.

Simlin thought of the children in the orphanage with

their steaming drinks, crescents of apple and their laughter. He curled up by the fire with his arms wrapped round his knees and sucked his thumb.

CHAPTER 12

INTO THIN AIR

Luka crept down from the attic and sat on the stair by the bakery door, listening to that woman talking about their mother. Her voice was like a saw, grating backwards and forwards. It twisted in the emptiness under his ribs. It hurt. Their mother had been taken away from them. She did not *want* to go. So she must hurt, too.

Luka could not bear it.

He had to find out if sly Vaskalia spoke the truth.

Early the next morning, he slipped out of bed. Jez was fast asleep. Even Dimitri was still wheezing like a bellows in his bedroom underneath the attic. It was just before dawn, the time when people have not intruded on the world, which is more than content to be without them. Nothing is fixed. It is a time of overlap.

It was the right time to change.

Luka felt his way downstairs. His stomach rumbled, but he knew not to eat breakfast on such a day. He must be clear-headed and ready.

He turned the key in the back door as softly as he could. Nobody must witness what was about to happen. He could not explain it to Dimitri or Jez, any more than he could tell his whole story to Aidan and the orphans.

Luka found the little wooden chair and placed it in the yard. He picked up his drum from the table, tucked it under his arm and perched on the chair. As he began to tap his drum with his fingertips, the swallows started to twitter and warble. Luka thought about making those tiny noises in his own throat.

He heard them swoop. What was it like, to fly? He pictured a swallow's streamer tail, and its body, swift and sleek, blue as midnight on the back and feathers pale as rosy dawn underneath. He stood up, spread his arms and curved them behind him like wings.

What would the world look like through a swallow's

eyes? Dimitri said their soft eyes were round and ringed with yellow. Their eyes were large for such small creatures, so their sight was good.

Luka would look through those eyes. He had escaped his blindness once and seen through the Cloud Cat's eyes. Now he would see through the swallow's eyes. There was no better companion for him when he was searching for something that had been taken away and hidden from him.

I know I can change myself. I know I have this gift. I can use it to search for my mother.

Luka sat down again. He picked up his drum and tapped it once. Again. He began to tap a rhythm, slow and soft but insistent, matching the rhythm of his pulse. On and on he played, drumming into a trance. The rhythm matched his heartbeat. Calm flowed through his mind and body.

He put down the drum and waited.

A soft wing touched his cheek. It happened again. Luka felt a rush of air as the birds swooped past him. One swallow came again and again. He knew it was a leader, guiding other birds across oceans and strange lands to be here in time for spring. A miracle bird.

Luka put his mind around it, and right into it, just as his mind had flooded into the Cloud Cat. He forgot about his breathing, forgot about his hungry stomach, forgot about the bakery, the orphanage, his mother, even his lonely brother.

And then Luka was cast out. There was no air and no light, no sound or breath. There was nothing. *I am lost. Am I dying?*

He struggled to get out of the emptiness.

Luka's body still sat on the chair in the baker's yard, like an empty costume, while his spirit vanished into thin air. *Sky shifter.*

CHAPTER 13

MIND LIKE A WATER WHEEL

J ez had been awake for much of the night, thinking about his mother. She was always just to the side of his mind.

Now his mind churned like the miller's water wheel. However much he tried to think of something else, he saw his mother's anguished face in the back of that truck as it drove away down that road, all those years ago.

Her eyes would not leave them. His mother's eyes were pale and light, neither blue nor green nor hazel. Jez's father said they were the colour of the leaves of an olive tree. Luka believed that her eyes were made of solid silver.

All through the fighting, people had vanished for no

reason. Jez did not want to think about where his mother might have been taken, or what might have been done to her. He was sure that he would never see her again, and so he tried not to let his mind wander, but now Vaskalia had stirred up that debris. Unhappiness and hope tangled together.

His father was gone. Jez knew the end of that story, and wished he didn't, but the brothers had never heard the end of their mother's story.

He buried his face in the pillow and cried himself to sleep.

When he woke, his head ached. A blade of sun cut through the skylight and pierced Luka's bed.

The bed was empty.

Jez raced downstairs. Dimitri and Big Katrin were sitting at the table downstairs, teapot and cups before them.

'Why didn't you wake me?' cried Jez.

'Slow down, Jez!' said Dimitri. 'You needed a lie-in after fixing the orphanage roof.' He grinned at Jez's early morning hair. It was sticking up, tufty as a scarecrow's. He reached out to ruffle it.

'Does it look funny?' mumbled Jez. 'Katrin . . . could

you cut my hair for me sometime, please?'

She nodded and poured him a cup of tea.

'And I need a shave,' he said, passing his hand across his prickly chin. 'Have you got an old razor, Dimitri?'

'Yes and you shall have it.' Dimitri yawned, stretching his strong little arms above his head, and Jez thought, It's all right for him. His chest is like a barrel and his arms are packed with muscles.

Dimitri said suddenly, 'Where's Luka?'

'He wasn't in his bed,' said Jez. 'I thought he must be with you.'

Jez found his brother outside, sitting on the little wooden chair, his eyelids closed.

Jez whispered, 'Luka? LUKA!' He tapped his shoulder.

Luka did not move. Panic flooded through Jez.

'Dimitri! Katrin! I can't wake him up!'

Dimitri hurried out. He peered into Luka's face and said , 'Let him rest,' hoping he sounded reassuring. Yet the depth of Luka's sleep was unsettling. It reminded Jez of that terrible moment when he found Luka unconscious in the cave with that white leopard.

They carried Luka up to his bed and laid him gently

down. Katrin put her hand on his forehead and thought how cold he was. She took hold of his wrist. His pulse was still beating, although it was slow.

'What'll we do?' whispered Jez, clawing his fingers through his hair.

'We'll leave him to recover,' said Dimitri. 'What happened to him out in the snow took more out of him than we thought. Letting him rest is all we *can* do. Get on with our work and leave him in peace.'

Big Katrin glared at him.

Dimitri shuffled from foot to foot. 'Don't look at me like that, Katrin. Of course we will keep watch over him. He's vulnerable. And I know someone who would take advantage of that. So, Jez, either you or I must always be in the bakery.'

In spite of his anxiety, Jez grinned. He said, 'I think Katrin is quite capable of dealing with Vaskalia if she comes back.'

CHAPTER 14

THE PATCHWORK BLANKET

Luka was free. He soared with the swallow. The invisible flicker of life that was truly Luka merged with the bird, flying with it, seeing what it saw. They flew high, where the air was thin and translucent with sunlight, and the earth shimmered below.

Luka remembered a blanket that his mother had made. It was a patchwork of coloured cloths. Luka had loved to run his hand across the blanket and feel each different one. There was rough hessian, soft velvet and wool, workaday cotton and even silk. His mother had sewn them together with green thread, in stitches that arched like bridges. He liked to trace the viaduct of stitches with his fingers.

He didn't know where the blanket was now.

From up here, the earth looked like that patchwork. There was the sombre dark green of a forest whose trees had shed their snow, the new green of woodlands and orchards, hedgerows washed with pink of blossom and buds and a field full of shining grass blurred with scarlet.

Somewhere beyond this is my mother.

They flew over the village. That tall house leaning out as if it would topple over was the bakery. Luka saw his skylight in the cat-slide roof, and the sandy blob pacing up and down the street, looking for him. There was the orphanage. In the roof was a gaping hole.

They flew above a little house like a pentangle. *Who lives there?* Up from the chimney twisted a spiral of acrid black smoke.

A squadron of geese beat past, in the shape of a great arrowhead, honking frantically. Luka saw their strong straight necks and smelled their hot feathery bodies as the swallow swooped out of their way and flew higher still.

A skylark approached from underneath. It battled on upwards, singing so strongly that its throat trembled with defiance and left a silver ribbon of song unravelling in the air below. Luka wanted to catch the song and keep it forever.

It must be an omen! It means I will find my mother, safe and sound.

Far below, a man and horse were ploughing. The turning earth was glossy brown. It dried in the sunshine, pink as the feathers on a chaffinch's breast. Across the sky sailed white clouds like clipper ships. The sky stretched wide open from horizon to horizon. How could anything be so *vast*?

Behind them rose the mountains, ancient beings with white hair and blue-green limbs. In his memory, Dimitri's voice murmured, *The further you stand from the mountains, the more clearly you see them.*

From up here the world looked as it should, as if it was at peace. There was no gunfire, no bloodshed and no fear. Up here, Luka understood that he had been given the power to help more than just himself.

Luka and the swallow danced in the sky, dipping and soaring among the clouds. Sky dancers. But they were the only ones who knew the steps.

CHAPTER 15

SEEING THINGS

Simlin crouched at the window of the five-sided house. He twitched the curtain with his nose and watched his mother stomping around her garden.

Mother stopped. She looked up at the sky and put up her mittened hand to shade her eyes. What was she staring at? Simlin tried to see. There was something little up in the sky. Something flying. Looked like one of those birds that flew to hot places for the winter. Simlin remembered that teacher blathering on about them, when there was a school.

Mother moved out of sight. At once, Simlin scooted across the cottage and reached up to the doll shelf. His hand closed around the seeing-ball. That blind boy was back in there again. Why? He was sitting on a chair. He wasn't moving. Something *else* was moving. It was curved, like a bow. It swooped up into the sky as if it was a crescent of dark moon.

Simlin's mouth hung open as he watched it. *Lovely lovely.*

Oh! Simlin realised with a start that the crescent of dark moon was a bird. It had a fork with two prongs for a tail. The blind boy had gone off in it.

But his body was sitting on the little chair.

He heard a rustling sound. Bone Cracker was moving up and down the rafter perch. Its bald head was cocked on one side. It was staring down at Simlin and the seeing-ball.

Simlin stuck out his tongue. Quickly he looked back into the ball. Swooping bird, swooping boy! Lucky little blind boy, swooping out there in strange places, seeing new things, and not shut up with –

The spit arrived before she did, hissing in the flames with a small green explosion and making Simlin think he had jumped out of his skin with fright.

'Give that to me!' she shrieked. 'It's mine! You've no right to look in there!'

CHAPTER 16

BLOOD RED CASTLE

The air became cloudy with dust.

I saw her in the city. In a window. Vaskalia's voice whined like a saw through Luka's memory. This was where his mother might be, in this unknown place, among strangers.

Luka thought that the city would be like his village, only with more houses. Instead, it spread out like a desert. There were buildings the colour of wet flour and they were broken. Their roofs were open to the sky. Luka saw crumbled staircases and sagging floors. Balconies clutched at the walls. In the middle of one wasteland was a vast crater as if a meteorite had crashed into the earth at lightning speed.

'That must have been a very big bomb,' Luka told the swallow.

The city changed as they flew nearer to the centre. Here, the houses that still stood were old, with timbers crossing their gables and roofs. *At the top of a tall timbered house . . .* Was she there?

Luka heard roaring. A tank with big caterpillar treads was bucking down an alleyway, making the houses tremble. The tank had no driver. Luka saw lorries and jeeps and more brown tanks. People hurried with their heads down. A lorry packed with soldiers ground along a potholed road. The soldiers held rifles as if they were spears.

Through the middle of the city flowed the wide river, until it split to flow round an island and join up again.

On this island sat a castle of stone. The stone was red, the colour of old blood.

Across the river stretched a wooden drawbridge lined with soldiers in battledress shadowed with brown and grey.

The swallow dived down and flew above the river.

'We haven't time to play!' cried Luka, but the swallow ignored him and swooped shockingly low, with its bill open, skimming the water, scooping it up and sipping so that Luka realised how desperately thirsty the bird had become.

And there was another feeling: hunger. The swallow turned and swooped back along the river, catching insects in its bill from just above the water as if it had a little fishing net. Luka was dimly aware of scratchy wings and jointed, stringy legs.

With its stomach full of insects the swallow flew straight along the river towards the blood-red castle.

'She won't be in there!' Luka cried, but the bird ignored him. It coasted above the drawbridge and over the battlements as if it knew where it was going.

Underneath the battlements, funny little forms hung upside down. They had old faces, wizened as gnomes. *Bats*.

The swallow swooped underneath the drawbridge and through the archway into a tunnel of darkness. Sluggish brown water sat in the stone. It barely moved. It stank. Luka saw green slime on the walls where dank water had slopped for hundreds of years. He heard the splash of a fat rat. He smelled excrement. Worse, he heard cries and the moaning of people in pain.

'I don't want to be down here!' he cried. The swallow ignored him.

Barely above the water were small windows. They were grilled with rusty bars. Behind them, Luka saw faces. A hand reached out as the swallow flew past and snatched towards its forked tail. Fast as an arrow, the bird flew under the castle and out of the other side, into the light. It circled the turrets, learning them, and flew close to the wall. Luka did not like this wall. The thick, crimson stone sucked everything into itself. He could hear nothing on the other side of it.

The swallow flipped into a courtyard in the centre of the castle. It swooped down to a single window, recessed deep into the stone. The window had wide sills and the thick glass was yellow with age and tobacco smoke, and netted with thick spiders' webs.

Here the swallow alighted. It began to feed on the tiny prisoners in the webbing, aphids and hoverflies, any small creature unfortunate enough to have flown into the trap.

Behind the yellowed glass were soldiers. Men in different kinds of battledress sat awkwardly around a long polished table, which reflected the faint daylight as if it were water. Above it drifted thick blue smoke from their cigars and cigarettes. So many different faces from many different tribes and places, ill at ease with each other.

At the top of the table sat a man in forest-shadowed uniform. On his chest gleamed buttons of gold, and epaulettes sat shining on his shoulders. His head was abnormally big. It was shaven and bumpy. He swung up his legs and put his boots on the table, boots as brown and glossy as the conkers on Jez's chestnut tree. The soles were clean.

He's the leader. But he's not from our land. He's from over the sea.

The man glanced quickly as a fox towards the window. In front of him was a pile of papers skewered by a metal spike.

At the other end of the table waited a small man, head down, shoulders drooping. Soldiers stood on either side of him. Luka realised that the small man was crying. The leader said something. Luka saw the gleam of his teeth. He waved his hand dismissively. A soldier took down a bunch of keys that hung on the wall behind the leader. The crying man was marched away.

The warlords shuffled in their seats. The shaven-headed man was sneaking glances all around him and Luka knew that he was trying to guess what the others were thinking.

The swallow picked one last insect from the sticky webbing. It flew away from the castle and over a market place. Two women stood behind a stall. Their faces were taut, as if the skin was stretched tight over wood like the skin on his drum. Their eyes were big and dark, the sockets deep in their gaunt heads. Luka looked at them and thought, Maybe it has been worse in the city. Maybe there's less food.

The women's stall had a few potatoes and a pile of cabbages, sliced open so that their middles gaped from pale yellow to dark green, like the contours on a map. All of a sudden, some boys about Jez's age ran forward and snatched up the food, stuffing it under their coats. The women cried out to the soldiers in their forest-shadowed gear lounging against a jeep. The soldiers shrugged. One of them laughed and spread his arms wide as if to say, *So what?*

The women took the few things that were left and hurried away. One of them was dabbing her eyes with her apron.

The swallow whizzed away from the market and along a small street. *Down a little winding way, at the top of a tall timbered house.*

It slowed down and flew level with the top storey of the houses. Luka thought that at last they would find his mother.

CHAPTER 17

SIMLIN'S GIFT

Simlin put his head down on his chest, to show her he was very sorry. If he did what she asked at once she might not punish him. He handed Mother the seeing-ball and waited, hoping that he looked as meek as a little lamb.

'What did you see in there?' she snapped. 'Tell me, droolgob!'

What can I get if I tell her? But straight away Vaskalia knew his thought and hit him hard around his head.

'*That's* what you can get for telling me!' she cackled. 'Don't try to bargain with me. Do as you're told. *Tell* me what you see!'

It hurt. His ears stung where she'd swiped them. If he

told her, she'd know his secret. She would know that he could see what was happening to the blind boy, and she'd never stop asking. So he kept quiet.

'Then I'll tell *you* what's happening, nincompoop! The big brother has gone to the city to find his mother. So the little one will be without his protection, for a long, long time.'

All Simlin could do was shrug, and think, She's got the wrong brother!

'That big boy likes his little brother so he protects him, like I protect you.'

Simlin frowned. That did not sound right. Out of the corner of his eye, he saw a big building loom in the seeing-ball. It was dark red as a scab of blood, a scab that you pick when there's nothing to eat. The swooping bird was flying near it, holding the invisible blind boy inside, keeping him tethered safe. And Mother can't see them!

Suddenly Simlin realised. He was just as good as any blind idiot! He had something special he could do. A gift! He made a *yip-yip-yipp*ing noise like a pig snorting. He had never made the noise before and he liked it.

'How dare you laugh at me!' yelled Vaskalia, twisting his ear.

Don't tell her, don't. But it hurt so much that he whimpered, 'Bird! Little bird! Bird with blue back and fork for tail.'

Vaskalia stopped twisting and began to gnaw at the copper bangles round her wrist. Her eyes swivelled as she plotted away to herself. She spat into the fire and stared at the lime-green flames. Then she looked up at the huddle on the rafter and whispered, 'Bone Cracker? Wake up, my dear. Off you go, into the night. There is something you must do.'

Bone Cracker dropped down and lumbered to the door. Before it went it glowered at Simlin over its shoulder. Simlin did not like Bone Cracker. It knew more than birds should.

Vaskalia busied herself around her pot on the fire, stirring, ladling. She passed Simlin a bowl with some hot liquid in it.

'Have a bowl of broth, sweet idiot,' she said. 'Drink this now. You *are* a clever droolgob. Cleverer than I thought!'

Clever droolgob? Sweet idiot? The words tumbled about

in Simlin's head. He tipped up the bowl and drank the hot broth. She was pleased with him! *He* was pleased with himself; he had not mentioned the blind boy.

CHAPTER 18

THE FACE IN
THE MIRROR

The city street was uneven, as if it had been picked up and shaken. One front door stood ajar. The next door was gone altogether. The windows were tiny and the rooms beyond them low and shadowed.

Somewhere, in one of these rooms, is my mother.

Through the first window Luka saw a room full of long boxes made of wood. One was broken open. Guns.

The next window had cherry pink curtains. Luka saw two small beds with bright knitted blankets. On each bed lay a teddy bear, but Luka knew that children did not sleep in this room any more.

In the next house, the attic was full of rubbish, a

tangled heap of clothes, a china mug with no handle, a battered suitcase and a broken cane chair. Not the kind of room his mother might live in.

But the next window was open! A net curtain billowed softly over the sill.

Luka could smell perfume.

At the back of the little room was the reflective pool of an oval mirror. A woman stood before it, lifting her long hair over her arm and moving the brush gently through it. Luka was transfixed. The brush flowed over the hair, as if the woman was casting a spell. Her face must be in the mirror. But the light was wrong and the window too far from the mirror. They could not see her reflection.

'My mother had long hair,' Luka told the swallow. 'And she had an oval face with such a soft curve to her cheek. Her skin was brown like Jez's. She had lips that turned up in a smile. And silver eyes, and a scar on her hand.'

The woman became aware that she was being watched. She stared intently into her mirror. She set down the hairbrush, turned, and walked towards the window.

'*Mum?*' whispered Luka.

The woman moved into the light. Her face was pale. Her eyes were very dark and deep with sadness. Under them were crescents of smoky tiredness, and lines ran down from her mouth as if her face had never worn a smile to smooth the lines away.

She opened the window further and leaned out, resting her elbows on the sill. She watched the swallow, without a flicker of any feeling on her face. Then she reached out and touched the swallow's back with a fingertip.

There was no scar on her hand.

The woman sighed. She withdrew and closed the window.

Disappointment flooded through Luka, so heavy that he thought they must drop out of the air.

There was one more house in the street. It was completely empty.

Everything has been burned on the fire to keep them alive during the winter, thought Luka. The floorboards had been pulled up. There were no doors left in the frames, no ghosts hovering in the rooms.

'Maybe there is another street with tall old houses, that looks like this one,' cried Luka. 'My mother could be there! Just once more round the castle, please. There may be a clue, you never know . . .'

So the swallow flew to the castle, up to the top.

And there on a turret stood Death, clutching his scythe. Behind him crouched ghastly figures, a man pointing a rifle, a weeping woman clutching a skinny baby, a skeleton, and children cowering from a figure wielding a stick. Behind them was a big clock.

They're not real, Luka told himself. They are made of wood blackened by fire, but where are the other figures?

The hands of the clock were stuck at midnight; the awful figures were left outside to haunt the city. Time was halted in the middle of war, pain, hunger and rage.

'Let's go!' cried Luka and the swallow looped the castle and set off straight above the river, only to be engulfed in a screaming black cloud.

'Oh Jez, I wish I was safe at home with you!' cried Luka as they were buffeted among the swarm of devils with needle tails, turning and tilting on sickle-shaped wings. Yet the swallow was not frightened. It was merely vexed by having to find its way through these sooty fiends. Swifts, dashing home to their nests, some of them already asleep. They were gone as quickly as they had arrived, but behind them was another agitation.

Way back down the river, the air was full of dark points, vibrating. They were coming nearer. Luka saw that the points had wings and made a soft sound.

'It's the bats! They're going out for the night. It's later than I thought . . . oh!'

Little birds should not stay out after dark.

CHAPTER 19

BONE CRACKER DROPS
ITS DINNER

It was the evening. Luka was still asleep so Katrin was still at the bakery. Usually she went home in the afternoons (although Dimitri wished she wouldn't) but this evening she wanted to stay and watch over Luka. Jez sat by Luka's bedside too, fretting.

Dimitri was secretly worried. He was sure he would find the old doctor in the inn down the road towards the sea. He could ask him about Luka.

'I'm going to the inn for a glassful,' he called up the stairs. 'I won't be long!'

Big Katrin had other ideas. She knew that Dimitri found it hard to have just *one* glassful, so she steered Jez downstairs to go with him.

Dimitri strode down the road towards the sea, singing in the late sunlight, with Jez slouching at his side. In the lush grass at the roadside bobbed wild roses pink as shells and creamy-white elder flowers, intricate as a lace collar on a woman's dress. Katrin should have a collar made of such lace, thought Dimitri, next to her rosy throat. He smelled smoke and saw that he had almost reached the little five-sided house with the tin chimney in the middle. His singing died away.

'I'm not frightened of you, Vaskalia!' he said, not very loudly. He thought he saw the curtains twitching and grabbed Jez's elbow as they hurried past.

A shadow passed overhead. It blotted out the golden evening and something round whizzed past Dimitri's face and crashed on to the road.

'Who's throwing boulders at us?' he roared, putting his fists up in front of his chest. He couldn't see anyone. Whatever made the shadow was gone. Dimitri looked at the boulder. It had four waving legs. He turned it over and stood it up.

'Well, hello there!' he chuckled.

'It was that big ugly vulture,' cried Jez, gazing up into the sky. 'Poor tortoise! That vulture dropped you to crack you open and eat you, didn't it? Like opening a tin of beans. Horrible thing has gone now!'

The tortoise blinked tiny eyes at them.

Dimitri sighed. He picked up the tortoise and said, 'You look like an Alfonso to me,' and slipped it into the pocket of his greatcoat. He wondered if tortoises got on well with kittens.

Tonight the inn was so full and noisy that only the people squashed near the door heard it open. Jez felt shy because he knew hardly anyone. Dimitri had not seen so many people in one place for months, and he knew most of them. There was the miller, the cobbler, the man who kept apple and cherry orchards, the donkey driver, Peter the Bus, a herdsman and a carpenter from the next village.

'It's wonderful to see you all!' he cried. 'Ah. And here's the man I want to see most of all.' Dimitri clasped hands with an old man with wispy white hair.

'Why do you want to see me? You look fighting fit,' said the doctor. He stared pointedly at Dimitri's stomach and said, 'But if you take my advice, you'll lay off the cakes and buns for a while. Is Katrin still looking after you?'

'Yes she is, I'm happy to say,' said Dimitri. 'Now, let me get you a glassful.'

When the innkeeper had set their drinks down before them Dimitri said, 'I want to ask your advice about Luka. You know, the boy who is almost blind? Gabriel and Evangelina's son? He ran away. And this is Jez, his brother, who found him and brought him home.'

'Brave boy!' said the doctor, taking Jez's hand and shaking it. 'So what's the matter?'

Jez said, 'Luka has gone very strange.'

'What do you mean? Has he a fever? Does he shake and have fits?'

'No. None of those things.'

'Then I don't know what you're worrying about,' sighed the doctor.

'This past day . . . he has . . . sort of disappeared from us. He is in a very deep sleep.'

'Perhaps he's tired,' said the doctor. 'There has been a lot to make him tired, what with the fighting and the long winter.'

The doctor ordered more glassfuls. Jez shook his head

– one had been enough for him. It was too sweet and burning.

The room grew hotter, the voices grew louder and Dimitri's voice got loudest of all.

'We live up here, minding our own business, growing food and making bread, for years and years, and look what happened!' he cried.

'What happened?'

'You know as well as I do, you stupid miller!' shouted Dimitri. 'People from one side of the mountain quarrelled with people from the other side about who owned a piece of rock for their goats! They fought. One of the leaders put himself in the castle. He got himself driven around in a big shiny car and locked up anyone he didn't like.'

'And he was replaced by another tyrant,' sighed Peter the bus driver, rolling up a cigarette. 'And he got another new car. We had a few poor harvests and everybody started blaming each other and fighting again and bringing up grumbles and resentments from long ago, and all the villages fought, and all at each other's throats!'

'The warlords took over!' cried Dimitri. 'They don't care about us, just their own power and wealth. They stirred up old resentments so all the villagers fought one another and nobody remembers why.'

Jez heard all the shouting, and felt befuddled. It all sounded crazy. Mad! *Old* resentments, he heard, and remembered Vaskalia with dread . . .

CHAPTER 20

THE GIANT CLAW

Simlin sat in a corner of the five-sided house, sipping his broth. Bat wing struts caught in his throat and he had to stick in his finger and drag them out, but the soup was warm and it filled a bit of him up. He thought longingly of the orphans with their biscuits, apple crescents and giggles.

It was dark now.

Simlin waited. The fire died. Bone Cracker did not come back. Mother had gone out, too. She would scream at him if the fire had died out altogether, because enemies and bad spirits could come down through the hole in the roof and not get burned to death. So he built up the fire, but not too much, because he had been in trouble for burning lots of wood last time she was out.

You never knew with Mother.

Simlin crawled on all fours to her elephant bed. It smelled of her so strongly: salty sea and rotten cabbage. Tonight there was another smell, too. Old flowers. He saw the box of powdery white stuff and the stick of greasy red and some yellow stuff in a bottle.

He sneaked his arm up the side of the bed and groped around under the rocky pillow.

He drew his hand back and looked at the tussock of dark hair. Curls. Clean, soft hair. *Must be the blind boy's hair. Mother will make special boy doll with real hair locks, and stick pins into painful bits.*

As Simlin pulled his arm back, he felt a sharp pain on his own skin, *ouch*! He stared down at a tear in his sleeve and watched scarlet blood well up and seep through as if it was a weave in a pattern. He put his arm up to his mouth and sucked the bleeding place. Had she made a Simlin doll? *Please no*!

He peered at the bed.

A claw was sticking out from under the mattress.

Simlin had never seen such a big claw. Whose was it?

With his mouth still fixed to his bleeding arm, Simlin backed away on bent knees until his back touched the wall and he could go no further. He stared at the claw. It moved!

Simlin stayed close to the wall all evening. He dared not doze. Whatever was under the mattress might come out after him.

The birthmark on his forehead began to tickle. Mother said it was a horrible ugly thing called a scorpion with a stinging tail that lived on hot rocks and horrible ugly children. The birthmark tickled Simlin because he was frightened of Mother.

And now there was a giant claw after him too.

CHAPTER 21

TALKING MAN

Jez was getting bored at the inn. The men were still rambling on and on and it was such a muddle!

'I never knew what they were fighting about!' grumbled a farmer. 'But somebody blew up the bridge so I couldn't take my beasts to market.'

'Everyone became an enemy to everybody else,' said Dimitri. 'One minute it was the way they prayed. Next minute it was if they ate chickens or geese, or if they washed their hair on Fridays or Sundays or their skin was a bit darker than the families in the next valley!'

'I never knew who they were,' said the farmer, 'but they didn't pay for my corn.'

'And then strangers came in big planes,' cried Dimitri, 'scaring our cattle and babies, and making a wind that swept all the fruit off our trees. The occupation. They've taken over but there is still fighting and shooting –'

'And looting!'

'And bombs!'

'And no electricity and not enough food and bad water, no post, no schools or enough medicine for the hospitals.'

'One day there wasn't even any bread!'

There was a moment's silence.

'That was not the war,' admitted Dimitri sheepishly. 'I had a problem with my yeast. I am sorry. But even that was because of quarrels way back. Old feuds between people. Different ways of life. Jealousies and spells . . .'

'We brought it on ourselves! The earth was punishing us all for our bad ways.'

'Listen to me!' roared Dimitri, leaping up on to the table. 'We are not to blame! Here we are, stuck in this ruined village that used to be so fine, so prosperous and friendly. The village children are orphans in an old school that's falling down round their ears. The occupation have repaired nothing, built nothing, and healed no one!

They've bombed our church, our houses, and even the ancient walnut tree.'

'No. That was the frost,' explained the orchard owner.

The landlord weaved his way through the tables with trays of glassfuls balanced along each arm. Dimitri took a glassful in each hand.

Oh no. Not more drink. Katrin will be so cross, thought Jez. He was getting so hot and tired that he thought he might explode. He wished they'd all stop shouting. He wished Dimitri would come on home. The baker swigged the liquid and hurled first one, then the other glass into the fireplace with a resounding *SMASH*! and stamped his boot so that the table rocked.

'We will re-build our lives!' roared Dimitri.

'Yes! Yes!' came the cry, making the old inn shake to the last of its rafters.

'We will demand money! Materials! Men! to rebuild the orphanage, and that is just the start!'

'That's right! Just the start!' they shouted.

'So it's everyone TO THE CITY!' bellowed the baker, red-faced, fists up in front of him, weaving and bobbing like a prizefighter.

There was a long pause. The old doctor spoke first. 'I am not shure that they will lishen to us. They will think we are a pheasant scrabble – peasant rabble – from the mountains.'

Everything fell quiet. There was only the fire crackling and Peter the bus driver burping.

'We should have a spokesh-shpokeman – a leader to shpeak for ush,' said the doctor. He returned to his glassful and drank deeply, smacking his lips while everyone waited, swaying in drunken respect. At last he spoke.

'It ish time for Talking Man. Every village used to have one. New Talking Man.'

'We've already got the right man for the job!' burped Peter.

'No we haven't!' roared Dimitri, swaying on the table.

'Oh yes we have,' said Peter. 'We've got you. *You're* our Talking Man. All those in favour of Dimitri?'

'Yes!' they shouted, waving their hands in the air. 'Dimitri for Talking Man!' They rushed at Dimitri, grabbed his legs and carried him off the table and round the inn.

'Oh no,' groaned Jez. 'Come on, Dimitri. We must get

back. I must look after Luka because Big Katrin will want to get home.'

'Leave him be, boy! Katrin will understand!'

Jez could not bear the hot, smoky inn a moment longer. He cried, 'See you, later, Talking Man!' and hurried out.

Dimitri thought he might be taking part in someone else's dream. He was not sure if he liked it. He allowed himself to be lifted down from the table.

'Now what have I let myself in for? I'm a baker, not a blinking politician! Put me down, boys. I have to get up early.'

He fumbled his way into his greatcoat, frowning as he felt a weight in one pocket. A strange little face peered up at him.

'Time to go home, Alfonso,' mumbled Dimitri and lurched off into the night.

But what was that? A voice was softly calling his name.

'Dimitri. Dimitri . . . Come over here. I have something for you. Something you want.'

CHAPTER 22

GHOST HEAD

Dusk began to fall as Luka and the swallow left the city.

'Everything looks different from the land we flew over this morning,' said Luka. This night darkness made him sad. He knew that when the swallow brought him back to his body, he would lose sight of the world again, and he had no chance of finding his mother.

'I said I wanted to find her for Jez's sake, swallow, but I wanted to find her for my own sake, most of all.'

He felt the swallow's response. It understood his feelings, but it was longing to get back to its mate. The bird's whole body strained towards home. It was tired, and struggling to concentrate on its flying, and Luka sensed that it was anxious. There was something not quite right about the air. The darkness felt as if it was holding its breath, waiting for something.

'Are you sure we are on the right course?' said Luka, again thinking how different the world looked. There was no visible moon. Luka could not see any outlines, or contours of the land. Everything had disappeared. They could be anywhere at all. The swallow dived down lower and the ground loomed up, indistinct. Luka glimpsed small, luminous clouds in the darkness and realised that it was white blossom in the hedgerows.

The swallow rose again to miss the trees and Luka sensed its fear.

And then he heard them, far away, but coming steadily nearer.

Wingbeats. Loud, deliberate wingbeats in the sluggish air.

'Don't worry, little bird,' Luka reassured the swallow. 'Only owls fly at night and I don't think they would catch you up here.'

The sky was full of dense cloud. Part of it glimmered with a yellow green light. More and more of this eerie light crept around the edge of the grey cloud. It was like a halo. It defined itself into the crescent moon. He saw it gleam on the feathers on the swallow's head, and light up something coming through the air towards them.

It's a ghost's head, thought Luka wildly. A head without a body.

The head had eyes ringed with white.

Long seconds passed. The moonlight fled away but they could still see the pale head flying steadily towards them. Luka saw that it was joined on to a body, after all. The body was carried on narrow pointed wings. The creature turned up towards them. Luka saw its white-ringed eyes with blank, fierce middles. He saw a hooked beak and felt the terror in the swallow, and the hot air moved by the relentless beating of its wings. *A vulture.*

Luka knew he had a reserve of great strength. He had willpower without fear. He urged on the swallow, putting his whole mind into its little body. Fly! Fly, away from the vulture! On to your home!

But the swallow was smaller, and so tired. And now it was flying for its life.

The ghost-headed bird opened its beak and let out a long thin scream.

Luka knew that eerie sound. With an awful clarity, he remembered what had attacked him when he stood up at the top of that gorge, just before he had fallen down into the Depths of Lumb.

This vulture wasn't after the swallow. It was after *him*.

CHAPTER 23

HOW DOES YOUR GARDEN GLOW?

Dimitri blinked into the darkness. He could not see who was calling him.

'Dimitri? I have a proposition to put to you. It is a matter of life and death…'

Dimitri tried to stand still.

'No, not *there*. We can't see each other. Come into my garden.'

Dimitri realised he had reached the five-sided house. Vaskalia's house . . . He heard rustling and snapping as she disappeared into the tangle of tall plants. Dimitri plunged in after her. A nodding lily tapped him on the shoulder. A jagged leaf scratched his hand. His knees were being nibbled and a fat soft moth bumped against his face.

Dimitri turned and blinked into the face of a flower with a luminous stamen curling like a chameleon's tongue. It was sticky and orange and it leered at him. He felt faint. He thought he would keel over in this garden. No one would ever know where he was and these plants would eat him. And the stars had fallen down on to Vaskalia's garden! The spearheaded grasses and long hairy leaves were spotted with tiny beacons that glowed and winked at him.

Vaskalia scuttled back to where Dimitri swayed queasily. Her face was lit green. She picked up one of the little stars, grabbed his hand and placed it on his palm.

'Why has it gone out?' he asked.

'Put it down and watch!' cackled Vaskalia.

Dimitri set it down on a leaf. The green glow reappeared. *Glow-worms.*

'She is shining to summon her true love!' cried Vaskalia. She leered up at him, fluttering her eyelashes. Dimitri saw that they were coated with black. She wore powder on her greenish cheeks. In his unsteady mind he saw Katrin's outdoor skin that shone with sun and wind and wished with everything he had that Katrin would come and save him.

'But why are they all here? Why are they in *your* garden?'

'Magical creatures are drawn to me, you see. I have a way with plants too,' she whispered. 'They could light the festival. It won't be long now.'

'What festival?'

'Don't tell me you're getting too old to remember!' she simpered. She sidled up to him, and even the night-scented flowers could not muffle her cloggy unwashed smell.

'I mean the midsummer festival, Dimitri. When we girls choose our sweethearts. I chose my sweetheart at midsummer, years ago. I chose Luka's father. Gabriel. Oh, what strengths our children would have had! We were the ideal couple, perfectly matched. But he resisted me and then *she* stole him! Luka's mother, the foreigner, she –'

'She was from somewhere else, that's all! She was from the other side of the mountain, from a different people!' shouted Dimitri. He felt as if he could scoop her rage up in big slimy lumps and hurl it far away. 'He married her, Vaskalia, not you. So stop it, will you? The boys' mother and father are both gone, through no fault of their own!'

She hissed, 'This year, there is a challenge at mid-summer.'

'What for? A midsummer queen? You? Ha ha ha!'

'No. An ancient ritual. It is the choosing of a special one.'

Something was stinging Dimitri's leg. He tried to move away but Vaskalia grabbed his elbow. 'Those brothers have moved in with you, haven't they, Mr Baker? But *I* could provide the perfect home!'

'They are both happily settled, Madam.'

'I am not talking about *both* of them,' she hissed. 'I want the little one. I understand his gift. He is no ordinary boy. From his dark past, there comes a terrible power. He must use it properly, and he is in danger where he is!'

'You're lying,' said Dimitri.

She said slyly, 'Dimitri, we all know I would be the perfect mother for Luka. His short life will be full of danger. *I* know what to do! *And* I would make it worth your while.'

She whispered, at length, into Dimitri's ear. The garden began to spin, taking Dimitri with it. He was whirling round and round, helplessly, with dreamlike flowers and lights and sickly scents. Why weren't there any *birds* in this garden? He heard words far away from him, words full of promise and delight . . .

Green glow-worm light illumed her face, making her eyes multi-coloured as opals, shining on her dark lips. She whispered. 'Go *on*, Dimitri! You know you want to! I have the knowledge and the power to make Katrin love you. With just one spell – or maybe two and a few pills – I can make that ogre Katrin forget all about Whassis-name who went off to fight. Think about it . . . A thick potion or two, pills in her tea, an incantation and fifty pins stuck in a doll of her man, and she's yours, Dimitri, she's yours!'

'I – I don't know,' he muttered, batting moths away from his mouth. Suddenly his head cleared and the nightmare lurched to a stop. Dimitri yelled, 'Listen to me, you! I won't betray Luka. He has Big Katrin to care for him, and he has Jez and me! Why don't you look after your own poor boy? Maybe he's special too! Spend a bit of time on him!'

At once he gasped and doubled up, clutching his belly

as if he had been stabbed. *Ow*! Another pain jabbed in his left temple.

He saw Vaskalia's face twisted with malice. 'You'll be sorry you ever turned me down, Baker!' she screamed, and Dimitri's heart missed a beat.

'Now what have I let myself in for?' he gasped as he lurched away out of the squirming garden.

CHAPTER 24

THE BLACK HORSE

Dimitri stomped in through the bakery door.

'Get me some coffee, fast!' he snapped at Jez. He pulled off his coat, was about to aim it at the hook high on the wall, when he stopped suddenly and took something out from his pocket and set it down on the floor. Then he glanced around and scowled.

'You haven't got everything out, Jez!' he ranted. 'You know I like it all waiting ready to bake the second I come downstairs!'

Jez did not risk saying that it was nowhere near the time yet. He set water to boil, and spooned coffee grounds into the jug.

'Luka still has not woken up,' he said.

Dimitri had his back turned to Jez. He rubbed his stomach round and round tenderly, as if he was trying to get a note from the rim of a glass. He started to pace up and down, hands rammed into his pockets.

Jez poured water on to the coffee. He waited for the coffee grounds to settle and brew. Why was the baker in such a mood? And what was that orange blotch on his cheek?

Suddenly Jez jumped back from the table and shrieked, 'There's something crawling around down there!'

'Eh? Oh – it's Alfonso the tortoise. At least it will be safe here.' Dimitri gave a little smile.

Jez said, 'I'm glad you rescued it. Look, the kittens are pawing its shell. They want it to come out and play. Now . . . here's your coffee.' As Jez watched, Dimitri yawned and stretched his arms above his head. 'Dimitri . . . how did you get your muscles? Your arms look so strong and mine just look puny. Luka teases me about them.'

Dimitri turned and looked at Jez as if he did not know who he was. Then something cleared on his face and he said, 'Sorry, I was miles away. And sorry I've been bad-tempered. I met Vaskalia on the way back from the inn. Or rather, she met me. Your brother will be fine, just fine.'

'What do you mean?'

'Oh, I'll tell you sometime.' Dimitri walked around Jez as if he was thinking of buying him. 'Why are you worried about your appearance all of a sudden? It couldn't have anything to do with that pretty young woman at the orphanage, now could it?'

Jez sank his chin down towards his chest to hide his blushes. 'I just think I should have a stronger body.'

'There's nothing wrong with you, Jez! We'd all like to be something else. Don't you think I would like to be as tall as you? Don't you think I'd like to look *down* at Katrin instead of up? The only way I can be taller than her is to stand on a chair with my baker's hat on.'

'That's another thing; my hair's *useless* too,' whined Jez, trying to smooth it down. 'I look like a hedgehog.'

'At least you've *got* some hair!'

'At least you've got good muscles!'

'Ah!' said Dimitri, sipping the coffee. 'I have a secret, Jez.'

'Please tell me!'

'All right, then. As you have made me such a good cup of coffee, I will.' Dimitri set down his cup and wandered into the larder, muttering, 'Now, where did I put them? '

He staggered out again with his weights and set them down on the floor by Jez.

'There!' he said. 'Now pick one up.'

Jez stared at the lumps of dark metal. He reached down. Dimitri shouted, 'No! Bend your knees or you'll hurt your back. Watch me.'

Dimitri's knees squeaked like mice as his legs bent. He reached down, shuddering, to pick up a weight in each hand.

'Wow! That's good, Dimitri!' exclaimed Jez. 'How far up can you go?'

Dimitri's teeth were clamped together in effort so that he could not answer. Sweat broke out on his nose and veins bulged blue on his forehead. He held the weights close to his chest for a few seconds, shaking and grizzling with the strain. Groaning like a bear giving birth, he raised them above his shoulders for a split second.

'Stop, Dimitri! Your eyes will pop out!'

Dimitri sat down on the floor, gasping for breath.

'Haven't done that for a while! Phew! But that's what made these muscles, Jez.'

'Lifting those lumps?'

'They're called weights, not lumps.'

Jez knelt by him, examining the weights.

'Where did you get them?'

'From the miller. He's got lots of them to weigh out his flour. The blacksmith welded two together with this strip of metal in the middle, so that I could grip them. To my specification, of course.'

'Of course.'

'You'll need to use them every day. Morning and night.'

'I will! I will!' cried Jez. 'They've certainly made you a fit man. Dimitri . . . I know this might sound nosy . . . but why don't you and Katrin . . . I mean, you make such a happy couple.'

Dimitri got up and busied himself with things for the morning, his yeast and flour. Jez fetched the jar of blue poppy seeds, set out the jug of oil, feeling as though he had said something wrong.

At last Dimitri said, 'Because Big Katrin is not free.'

'What do you mean, not free?'

'Katrin was married. She believes she *is* still married. At the beginning of the fighting, her husband saddled up his little mountain horse. He loaded it with food, blankets, his rifle and some ammunition. He kissed Katrin goodbye. Then he rode off to join the freedom fighters in the forest.'

'And?'

'A few weeks later, the horse came back. Alone. Katrin has not seen her husband since. She keeps the horse in the field by her house.' Dimitri sighed and his eyes filled with tears. 'She has not spoken one single word since.'

Jez had never thought about Big Katrin's life before. She just turned up at the bakery, smiled, made cakes and spoiled children. How little he knew about people's lives. *Katrin*.

CHAPTER 25

ICE ROUND YOUR HEART

'Fly faster! Higher! We can do it! We can!' insisted Luka, but his hope was flagging. He feared the exhausted swallow might burst with the effort. Only a few days ago, it had arrived from its flight over thousands of miles across the sea. It was already tired, before this journey to the city and back.

Below them flapped that ghost-headed bird. It was not going to give up.

What would it feel like to be torn to pieces?

Luka thought of nothing except escape, but somewhere there was searing pain, and somewhere there was breath, wheezing and shrieking. They were failing!

They were losing height, losing speed, losing strength.

The swallow flipped and flew straight upwards. Luka felt fear flood its small body and set like ice around its heart. All it could do was climb and hope to lose that vulture that was waiting for them to fall to their deaths.

Far below them Luka glimpsed lights, as small and soft as fireflies. They disappeared almost at once.

They must be the lamps and candles from the village. The orphanage. The bakery. We'll never see them again! But we'll have to fly onwards. If we lose height trying to get back to the village, that vulture will have us.

'Keep flying high, swallow. Head for the mountains!'

CHAPTER 26

DIVE-BOMBING
THE BAKER

Early next morning, the swallows whirled over Dimitri's yard as if he had hurled a handful of little anchors up into the sky. Every so often, they swooped down, dive-bombing the baker so that he had to wear his hat, which was a shame because he liked to feel the sunshine on his bald patch.

He stacked the wood into the wheelbarrow and took it inside, dumped the logs in the basket and turned to Jez.

'Has Luka woken yet?'

'No. He hasn't stirred at all. That makes it a long time. No, let me lift the trays, Dimitri.'

'Jez, I'm sure young Imogen likes you, with or without

big muscles.'

'It's nothing to do with Imogen!' insisted Jez, blushing. 'I just – well, I like to be fit and ready for anything.'

Into Dimitri's unwilling mind came that face full of cunning lit green by glow-worms. 'You'll *need* to be ready for anything, Jez.'

'What do you mean?'

'I mean,' said Dimitri heavily, 'that there is a burden your family has to carry, Jez, and you may well have to shoulder some of it.' He busied himself putting cinnamon bark into a pestle, muttering, 'It's time I made some cinnamon buns . . .'

'Stop changing the subject, Dimitri! *Please* tell me what Vaskalia was up to last night!'

'All right. Vaskalia wants Luka to live with her. She wanted me to hand him over to her.'

'Over my dead body!' shouted Jez. He stormed across the bakery and kicked the oven hard. He spun round and glared at Dimitri as if *he* were the enemy.

'Jez, Jez . . . Vaskalia claims she knows all about your family. Things that the rest of us don't know . . . And she promised me things.' Dimitri caught his breath as he recalled Vaskalia whispering secrets in his ear.

Dimitri became aware that someone else was watching him. He spun round with a guilty look on his face. 'Katrin – you gave me a fright!'

She crossed to the table, picked up a mug, tapped it and glared at Dimitri as if asking him a question. She had heard everything.

'No, Katrin, I didn't let Vaskalia make me a drink. No, er, not this time,' he said.

Katrin placed the mug back on the table. She looked into Dimitri's eyes for a long moment and Dimitri's face slowly blushed dark as a plum. Katrin went upstairs to make some tea and Jez whispered, 'Dimitri, what's going on? What did Vaskalia promise you?'

'She offered me Katrin. She said she could make Katrin fall passionately in love with me if I gave her Luka.'

'Oh no, Dimitri! Please say you didn't agree!'

Dimitri flung himself down at the table and hid his face in his hands. When he took his hands away Jez saw tears in his eyes, and felt a stab of hurt. Dimitri was so strong and good-humoured – what could make him weep?

'Jez, I am ashamed to admit to you that I was tempted.

I still am . . . I love Katrin. I want her to share my life. But –'

'But?'

'But do you think she would love me if she thought I had betrayed you two? You're like my sons! Would Katrin stay five minutes with me if I handed Luka over to that woman? No. And I would never forgive myself. So . . . Vaskalia knows she's getting no help from me.'

Before Jez could stop himself, he put his arms around the little baker and gave him a big hug. He said, 'Katrin cares about you *anyway*. You're such a great guy! Maybe one day she'll fall in love with you without Vaskalia's meddling.'

And please never change your mind. Please never let Vaskalia get Luka in her clutches.

CHAPTER 27

BATTLE OF THE BIRDS

Luka saw a dark angel soaring in the sky. It was flying towards them. It was haloed in gold. The sheen glowed all round its body. It was bearing down on them, nearer and nearer. Luka saw its majesty. He was caught in the dark centre of its golden eye.

A golden eagle!

Luka and the little swallow did not stand a chance. Between this awesome eagle and the vulture below, they would be pulled apart.

The eagle beat towards them. The little swallow rocked on the air wash of its flight. Luka saw its clear golden eye and realised that the dark centre was not fixed on them at all.

It was hunting the ghost-headed bird below.

The eagle dropped from the sky, straight as a machete cutting sugar cane. The two creatures knotted together, turning over and over, as if beaks and wings and claws belonged to one turning bird.

The bewildered swallow darted to and fro through clouds of feathers. It was as if someone was slashing pillows open with a knife, smothering the birds in a storm of down and feathers. Beads of bright blood fell to the earth. Wings thumped, beaks ripped flesh, and Luka heard the eagle's yelp, such a thin sound for such magnificence, and the thin scream of the ghost-headed bird.

In between them was the swallow, like a helpless piggy in the middle.

CHAPTER 28

BOWLFUL OF SNOW

After the terrible screaming and tearing of the fighting birds, the silence of the mountains was profound.

Luka woke to silver light streaming into the crevice. Outside, the sky was azure blue behind the clear peaks. Below was a hollow, filled with snow, as if someone had filled a shallow bowl full to its brim.

Some of the snow began to move. White creatures with long ears chased in a circle. At some unseen signal they turned, and chased in the other direction.

Mountain hares. Hundreds of them, bounding in the sun, on long thin legs. But up in the crevice, Luka's

· 128 ·

swallow did not move. Luka could not feel it breathing.

'You have pushed the bird too far.'

That voice. It was the same voice Luka had heard in the cave, when he ran with the Cloud Cat. Now he smelled the scent of burning wood, juniper and birch, and remembered that he had smelled wood smoke in the cave. Luka thought of his dream of the man with the hair of frost. That golden-faced man carried a bundle of twigs on his back. With a piece of iron and a pinch of tinder, the man had conjured up a spark, and at once a fire leaped. Down the mountain bounded the Cloud Cat to wind herself around him.

This morning, Luka saw no one, but the voice was everywhere. It echoed in the wind that blew constantly around the mountaintops. The words echoed each other as if they were notes of music.

'You chose well, Luka. Yes, you chose the right creature. Yet you did not love him enough to think of his needs.'

'But swallows fly thousands of miles, and –'

'You drove him too hard. You expected of him even more than you expected of yourself. Reckless boy!'

'I'm not!' shouted Luka, but the voice ignored him and

went on, 'You searched on and on for your mother, and risked the swallow's life.'

'I didn't mean to!'

'You did not think through with *his* mind. You exhausted his small body and drained his energy. You fed on it. Now he may never fly home again.'

'But the eagle came to save us!' cried Luka.

'The eagle did *not* come to save *you*. The eagle came to protect his nest and his larder from that bird which flies near his territory. Why should the eagle care about people?'

Luka sobbed, 'I did not find my mother!'

'No. You may have found other things.'

'I haven't found anything!' shouted Luka angrily. 'What good is this gift if I can't even get my mother back?'

There was no answer.

He stared out at the mountain bowl. The hares played as if nothing was different. For a moment he heard the mournful howl of the wolf choir. The howl died away into a terrifying silence. Luka felt as if the voice had reduced him to nothing. He was worthless.

When the voice spoke again it was softer, and came from a different part of the mountain.

'Your ancestors made spirit journeys in different creatures. Now they talk to you, passing on their thoughts and stories and their understanding. You can take from them whatever you wish and pass it on.'

'What do you mean?' cried Luka. 'I don't think you old ancestors know what the world is like any more! Terrible things have happened and you don't understand them!'

'Luka. Perfect your precious gift. Bring life back to your village. Work on your changing and learn. Others share a little of this power, other people you may know.'

'Who?' cried Luka.

Again the voice ignored his question and continued, 'There are others who do not have the gift but want it. Beware! You are always in danger from them. Your family and those nearest to you are in danger too.'

Luka thought, Nobody has told me this before. Yet I suppose I knew about it. That's why I went off in the snow after the Cloud Cat.

He said, 'What must I do? Won't you tell me anything?'

'Use the gift, or it will vanish. The gift is for everyone but it speaks through you. Give people back their lives. Help them to learn to love the world again and find its joy.'

The echoes of the words tumbled against each other and fell like dominoes.

'See the Cloud Cat? Take your strength from her.'

On the mountain opposite, the Cloud Cat padded along a narrow ledge. Her shoulder blades slid under her luxuriant dappled fur. Two small cubs trotted at her side.

She stopped. She stared across the chasm with her gold nugget eyes. She knew he was there. Luka felt himself pulled into those eyes. He was lost in their worlds of wildness.

Later he remembered where he was and what had happened and begged, Please don't let the swallow die! And if it should die – what will happen to me? How will I ever get back? As he watched the Cloud Cat, strength eased into him, warming his body. The frail swallow began to breathe light and fast with him. It was panting, its tiny chest rising and falling, its beak open. The bird was so *thin*. It shuffled to its small awkward feet. It stretched out its wing and began to preen its cobalt blue feathers ready for its flight home.

'But first, little bird,' Luka said, 'you must eat and drink and get strong.'

CHAPTER 29

MERINGUE CLOUDS

Big Katrin strode to work without her scarf. A gentle wind lifted her oak-brown hair. The little clouds in the sky were puffy as egg whites whipped for meringue, and Katrin felt a spring in her step and a desire to smile. Everything was going to be better, and she wondered if she had been too hard on Dimitri the day before.

She opened the bakery door on to a nervous silence. The loaves were lined up on the trays ready to be baked. Dimitri and Jez hovered by them, fidgeting.

Katrin hid her smile as she marched past them and on up the stairs to make tea.

Jez and Dimitri relaxed, listening to the water filling the

kettle, the cups and pot put on the tray. Things were as they should be again. They waited to hear the kettle whistle.

Then they heard Big Katrin cry out. No words, just an exclamation of joy.

Luka was awake.

At once, he wanted to go to the orphanage to tell his story to the children.

'Of course you can,' said Jez, grinning with relief. 'We'll go after the baking.'

Jez looked at the children sitting all around Luka. Their eyes were smudged and dark. Those eyes had seen so much to make them mistrustful. Now they were full of hope as they waited for Luka's story.

'And about time too!' cried Aidan, shuffling his bottom around on his cushions. 'I have had to wait ages and *ages* for the next instalment. Where did you go *this* time?'

Aidan puzzled Jez. He seemed to know more about Luka's stories than he should.

'I went high into the sky, with a swallow. And it was like dancing!' cried Luka, spreading his arms wide, lifting his face up to the orphanage ceiling. 'I was the Sky Shifter.

The swallow and I danced through the clouds. Over them, under them, round them and through the blue, blue sky. I saw the earth far below. Like a beautiful patchwork blanket, with woods and fields and a horse and shining water. I saw the village, and the bakery *and* the orphanage. They are so small, you know.'

'Did you see me, Luka?' cried Erin, jumping up and down.

'No, I didn't, I'm afraid. I think you were still in bed.'

'What was the best bird up there?' asked Ellie.

Luka put his head on one side. 'One of my favourites was the skylark. She shot straight up, VOOOM! She was so small, but she sang such a big song. A rippling song, spinning up in the sky.'

He paused and Aidan began to drum his fingers impatiently on the arm of his chair. Luka could hear Aidan's drumming, and something else too. There's that whispering again. '*Milksop, idiot, saphead . . .*'

'The swallow was kind to take you, wasn't he?' asked Ellie.

'Yes, he was,' said Luka quietly. 'And he was the very best bird of all.'

'*Bam Bam Bam! Boom Boom!*' shouted Florin, cheek flat to the piece of wood he was aiming at Luka so that Luka jerked his head away, startled.

'Did you see any penguins?' asked Daniela.

'No. No penguins up there. But I saw swifts. And bats.'

'Were there any big birds?' asked Ellie.

'Yes. There was – there was an eagle. Soaring and gliding, like a dark sail with gold all around. It was magnificent. Its great wings beat like slow drums.' Luka shivered. He did not say more, because it would frighten the children. He did not want to remember that horrible fight.

Upside down in the rafters, Simlin hissed, '*Idiot . . . Idiot! Wonder if Bone Cracker was in your story, idiot?*'

'Luka! Luka!' nagged Aidan, like a terrier with his teeth in a trouser leg. '*Why* did you go flying off up in the sky with a swallow?'

Luka hung his head. Aidan always asked the questions he did not want to answer.

'Come on!' persisted Aidan.

'I was looking for someone.'

'Who? Did you find them? Maybe it was your father!'

Luka could not answer. He wanted to cry again. That spiteful whispering had not gone away, and if his mother really was in the city, he had failed to find her. *Failed.* He did not want Jez to know who he had been looking for. So he just shook his head.

Why did that woman tell Jez she had seen our mother in the city? Again he heard the voice telling him, Others want your gift . . .

CHAPTER 30

STRANGERS

Luka sat in the sunshine next morning, listening to the swallows. He remembered the grinding engines of lorries and tanks in the city and the rifle fire. He had heard no birdsong, and no music. His gift had made him realise that he loved his quiet village and the people he knew.

He had not dreamed of his mother this morning. Usually he met the gleam of her silver eyes when he woke, but not today. Did that mean something bad? Was it an omen, meaning he would never find her? He tightened up his face against that other pain which Aidan had stirred. *His father*. Luka was not going to think about his father. He was not going to remember even *having* a father.

The door from the bakery was flung open.

'Yeah! Here I go!' shouted Jez, springing into the yard. Luka heard him ripping off his shirt, followed by the grunts, footfalls, bounces and curses of Jez's exercise routine which now happened in any spare moment. Luka heard the clanging of the weights on the ground, and groaning and cursing as Jez lifted them.

He heard the latch of the yard gate and the hubbub of children on the other side, Imogen's voice and Jez's mumbled 'Uh – hullo . . .' as he fumbled to pull his shirt back on.

'Come on inside, Imo,' said Luka, getting up and reaching for her hand. 'And you lot, just don't scare the swallows!'

'Bossy Luka!' cried Aidan.

'Behave yourself!' Eva told him.

'We were out for a walk and so we thought we'd call in,' said Imogen. Then in a lower voice she said, 'Some people came to the orphanage, Jez . . .'

'What people?' asked Jez, steering her into the bakery, where Katrin and Dimitri were sitting at the table with the coffee pot.

'Two men and a woman. They tried to push their way inside but Eva fastened the chain across the door. Said they wanted to take some children with them, that they had lovely new homes for them. I did not trust them one little bit. They said they would be back.'

'Imogen, I'll build a real home!' cried Jez. 'For now I'll fix more locks and –'

'– and you had better fix the hole in the roof too,' said Luka.

Jez stared at him. 'How could *you* see a hole in a roof?' he chuckled. Luka shrugged.

'Jez, I have to go the city soon,' announced Dimitri. 'I'll buy tools and materials for you.'

'Why are you going there?' asked Jez.

Dimitri fiddled with his coffee cup, swirling the grounds round and round. 'To buy a van. Now that Katrin has started baking cheese pies again, there's even more produce to deliver. Business is booming. People are returning to the village to start their lives again. You're good with your hands, Jez. You could carve like your grandfather did.

'There is something all of you should know.' Dimitri

pushed his cup away and stood up to face them. 'I have been chosen as Talking Man for the village. I must tell the world we need help.'

Luka felt his way over to Dimitri and took his hand. He said, 'Then you must go to the dark red castle. And fix the midnight clock to make everyone feel better. And Dimitri, please play lots of fiddle music! I want to dance. And I want you to sing, Eva!'

That's what the voices meant. I can see things, and understand them, for everyone!

Jez's stomach was beginning to feel bad again. How could Dimitri afford a van? Had Vaskalia been giving him money? And now Luka was talking oddly again.

'But you've never even been to the city, Luka!' he wailed, shaking his head. His face blanched with fear, like an almond slipping its brown skin in hot water.

Luka's lips turned up in that secret little smile that drove Jez mad. It was as if Luka was going somewhere without him, somewhere dangerous.

And now look at him. Dimitri had fetched his fiddle. Eva sang. And Luka danced all around the yard.

CHAPTER 31

GANG OF GHOSTS

Simlin ran fast as a hare back from the orphanage. The five-sided house was heaving with a strong meaty aroma. Not bat soup, a different smell that made Simlin want to eat and eat and eat.

'Ah! So there you are, my child!' Vaskalia said in a pleasant voice that Simlin had never heard before. Who was she talking to? Simlin glanced furtively behind him, but no one had followed him in.

What was Mother cooking in the big black pot?

Simlin took a step towards the pot. His body said, *No! She'll smack hard!* But his nose led him there.

Mother cackled, 'I feel like cooking a lovely feast

today! Guess what's in my stew?'

He smelled and blinked and whispered, 'Orange carrots . . . tatties . . . matoes and onions . . . green bits and . . .'

Mother took over. 'Good herbs and spices. Green peppercorns and salt from the sea.' She ladled brown stew into a spare tortoiseshell bowl.

Simlin sniffed hard. The scorpion on his forehead itched *oooooscratscrat*. But the smell from the cooking pot was so tempting and the rumbling in Simlin's tummy so shuddering that he did not scratch his scorpion but held his hands out ready.

In the middle of the gloopy stew was a huge wedge of something. Was it a chicken? Simlin had seen chickens strutting around the village this springtime. They wore wobbly rubber bits on their heads. He had never eaten one.

But chickens were not giants.

Simlin drooled as he looked at the huge wedge. Was it a leg or a piece of wing? Perhaps it was a goose from the common land? A goose would stab Mother in the bottom with its big hard beak, rather than let her pick it up. He pictured Mother running, bosoms flopping, to get away from them. And he felt it beginning in his chest. *Yip yip snort, yip yip snort* . . . But better not laugh *yip yip snort* in front of Mother.

He snatched up the wedge of flesh from his bowl and sank in his teeth. *Mmmmm*! Never had Simlin tasted anything so rich and so tender! His fingers slid around on the greasy hunk, fingers to lick later.

Mother watched with her head on one side as Simlin tore bird off bone and drank broth, tatties and all, from the bowl, wiped face with back of hand.

'More?' said Mother. Yes. Two bowlfuls more! But when she asked the next time, Simlin shook his head. Suddenly he had eaten too much and felt very sick.

She grabbed his wrist. Her rough thumb and third finger met around it. She cooed, 'But we need to build you up! Make you strong! All ready for the challenge. I shall feed you and fatten you, Simlin. Fatten you right up!'

She threw back her head and laughed so that her wattles wobbled. Simlin heard that high note in her cackling that meant *hurt*. He saw the cold flints in her eyes. His scorpion mark began to itch terribly. Mother stopped laughing and looked at him again. Simlin liked it better when she ignored him. But he had to ask her, 'What challenge?'

Mother hissed, 'You've got some secrets from me, haven't you? Well, I've been keeping something secret from you for a long time too. I have something for you . . . if no one else gets it first! It will be a challenge to see who gets it!'

She stomped over to the bed. *Oh no! The claw!*

Squat as she was, Mother was heaving-strong. She braced herself, grunting, and with her fat little arms she heaved up her mattress on to its side. There was jangling and cracking and a rotten stinky fishy smell.

'Look! Look!' she crowed. 'Look what's underneath!'

Simlin thought at first the mattress had been lying on an enormous ghost. He saw a white skin, bigger than any creature he had even dreamed of. On it hung dead creatures. A long curling snakeskin, crazed like cobblestones. An old wing of brown feathers. A hooked beak. Yellow tombstone teeth. A pair of empty shells. A thing with dangling tentacles. A flatfish with empty eye sockets and a herringbone fringed with spikes. Dried wings, teasel combs. Bits of rusty chain and a curved knife. The mangy long tail of a great cat. At the top of the ghost shape were the antlers of a stag. Tatters of velvet hung ripped from them. And that giant claw . . .

'The shaman's cloak!' she cackled. 'So heavy! So weighty I will need a fine strong donkey to carry it. This is the cloak of the one whose spirit changes. This is the cloak of he who dances in and out of creatures, and in and out of people too. Why not? *Why not*! Whoever wears this will be the Powerful One!'

She stroked the cloak – what was it made of? Fur? Greasy hair? Skin?

'The cloak has its ghosts!' she whispered. 'Its very own gang of ghosts! All those who have worn it trail behind the one who wears it. All those whose lives have been changed. All those creatures too, dead or alive . . . Who will wear it next?'

Simlin wanted the ground to open so she could not see him. But the ground stayed shut.

'Whoever wears it must be strong, my son!'

Simlin shook his head so fast he thought his teeth would fall out. *Not me, not my cloak.* He knew that cloak was bad. It reeked of horrible things. His fingers scratched at his scorpion mark. *Don't want to wear big stinking cloak, never ever!* He scuttled away and crouched in a corner, plotting, face blank so that Mother would not know. *Little boy . . . orphans and ladies . . . Mother . . . bad smothering cloak.*

And it came to Simlin what he must do. *Get rid of that blind boy.*

The tail of the scorpion on his forehead whipped over to sting, then cooled and lay still.

CHAPTER 32

TIME TO GO

Big Katrin set out plates ready. She was making little butterfly cakes. The buns were already baking in the oven. She had her sharp knife to hand, ready to slice off the tops, cut them into butterfly wings and wedge them to the cakes with butter icing and lemon curd.

She began to mix pastry for cheese pies. They were proving popular. Her plump hands with their fine tapered fingers flew lightly through the butter and flour.

As she worked, she remembered what her mother had told her when she was a little girl. Sometimes people were born who could see into different spaces. They were special, rare beings. Their spirits could move out of their own bodies and into other creatures, as if they were changing clothes. Born storytellers, they were in special sympathy with the earth and its energy, in a way that others were not. They had the gift of loving life and passing this gift on to everyone else in their stories.

The villagers respected these wise storytellers. The gift was various. Some could heal, help sickness of mind and body, and guide people in time of trouble. Katrin's mother said such people had always lived in the mountains, and round about. When they died, their presences stayed behind to help everyone, and lived on in people's minds.

But that was only part of the story.

They could destroy themselves. And others. Their families were in danger. Others wanted their power. They could cause jealousy as well as love. There was no certainty that they would use their gift for good.

Such people were dangerous, because they were so reckless.

Especially if they were motherless children like Luka.

Big Katrin mused over what Vaskalia had told her that day, after she had turned the yeast and milk sour. Vaskalia said that this gift came from Luka's father's family.

Vaskalia was consumed with jealousy because she had wanted it for her own son Simlin. Yet try as she might, Katrin could not recall her mother ever saying that Gabriel's family had the gift. Luka was the gifted one, Katrin knew. He had a way of absenting himself from the everyday world where the rest of them lived, and then returning more alive than before. He had extreme empathy, and imagination in bucketfuls! And he had joy.

How could a small blind boy be the wise one who saw for everyone? Katrin was sure he was. She had seen him in that glass ball, because she, too, had awareness and could see certain things. Katrin knew she must watch over Luka and make sure Dimitri protected him like a father.

Katrin smiled as she thought of Dimitri. *He* certainly had no spirit gift. Katrin did not see it in Jez either, but they were there to love and support Luka. She remembered Luka dancing to the fiddle when he had been brought out of the snow. He heard the joy of the universe and would bring it to the others. He had led the children this morning, dancing in the yard to Dimitri's fiddle and Eva's singing. No one but Luka could have persuaded Eva out of her sadness to sing in the yard.

Outside, the swallows twittered and trilled around the children's heads. Syrup the cat rolled on her back and dreamed of catching one. The pupils in her green eyes narrowed to arrow-slits in the sunshine. Her kittens hid, pouncing on shadows.

The children clambered in and out of an old barrel-shaped wagon leaning against the woodshed. Dimitri had found it abandoned on the road to the sea. He was going to paint it. Lisa woke up the dog and tried to make her chase after sticks. Eva sat Aidan in Dimitri's wheelbarrow and from there he directed the games in his imperious voice. Maria sat with the tortoise on her lap, stroking its shell. Florin found a stick in the woodshed and crept around the yard with it, going *neowm BANG aaagh!* and falling on his side, hand clutching his throat.

Luka stood in the doorway and heard their play. He did not try to join them.

Jez touched his arm and said, 'Poor kids! I'm going to build them somewhere better, but I need *money* and help to do it. And you need to rest, Luka. Don't go far from home.'

Luka murmured, 'Don't worry, Jez.'

He was glad he did not have to live in the orphanage. He knew he was lucky living in Dimitri's bakery with Jez. He also knew now that he could use his gift to help to make a better home for Imo, Eva and the children, even for taunting Aidan. But . . .

He grabbed Jez's hand and cried, 'I need your eyes.'

'You've always had them, silly! You drive me bonkers, Luka.'

Luka smiled. He loved to tease Jez and make him cross, but he needed him because he was set apart. What about those whispered names? And Aidan sticking words where they hurt. *A father* . . . He would not think of that. *A mother*. He had failed to find her. That vulture.

The voices had said he must share his gift. They made him mad, always telling him what he should do! Now he understood a little of what they meant. He could see things that other people could not, see the energy in the earth, and he knew about the blood-red castle, the warlords and dungeons. He could not change the world on his own, but he could help Dimitri be Talking Man. He could help Jez mend the orphanage, and make the children want to live in the world again.

Luka put his mind towards the Cloud Cat. He daydreamed of her with her two blue-eyed cubs. As he did so, he saw the river again, and the mountain ledge. And the *cave* . . . That was it! If only he could find it again.

First he must rest. He smelled the cakes turning golden in the oven, and licked his lips as he thought of the creamy butter icing and cool sweet lemon curd.

In a few minutes, Katrin would be calling them inside. So for now, Luka went into the yard to play.

TO BE CONTINUED . . .